THIEF GIRL

Victorian Romance

FAYE GODWIN

Tica House
Publishing

Sweet Romance that Delights and Enchants!

PERSONAL WORD FROM THE AUTHOR

Dearest Readers,

I'm so delighted that you have chosen one of my books to read. I am proud to be a part of the team of writers at Tica House Publishing. Our goal is to inspire, entertain, and give you many hours of reading pleasure. Your kind words and loving readership are deeply appreciated.

I would like to personally invite you to sign up for updates and to become part of our **Exclusive Reader Club**—it's completely Free to Join! I'd love to welcome you!

Much love,

Faye Godwin

VISIT HERE to Join our Reader's Club and to Receive Tica House Updates:

https://victorian.subscribemenow.com/

PART I

CHAPTER 1

Ivy clutched her grandmother's skirt, the cheap material rough and dirty in her little hands. She tried her best to hide behind Granny's legs, but a withered hand closed over her shoulder, and she found herself being pushed forward.

"Come on, child," hissed Granny. "Stop your foolishness."

Ivy whimpered, pulling up a piece of Granny's skirt to cover her face. She didn't know the woman who was standing on the doorstep, and she didn't want to, either. She just wanted to go back to her corner of the kitchen and curl up on her blanket and sleep. But she couldn't tell that to her grandmother.

"Do you see what I have to put up with?" said Granny, exasperated. She straightened, loosening her grip on Ivy's shoulder. "I don't know what's the matter with this child. She hardly speaks a word or looks at anyone. She's no use to me whatsoever."

"Oh, Mama, is that really the point?" asked the woman on the step.

Now safely hidden behind Granny's legs, Ivy dared to peer around her knees, giving the woman a quick glance. She was scrawny and weathered; her face so brown and wrinkled that it looked like a piece of old leather that had been left out in the sun for too long. Her lips were chapped, and her gnarled hands were roughly wrapped in bits of rags. She had them planted on her hips, and her filthy hair seemed to be a dull shade of red beneath the coating of grime that covered her from head to toe. Ivy didn't dare to look at her eyes.

"The point, Bertha, is that I'm much too old to be running after you girls," Granny griped. "You both were supposed to have provided for me in my old age. Worked my fingers to the bone, I did, trying to get you two some kind of a future or even an education." She snorted. "And look where that got me. One daughter comes home pregnant, gives birth to the child, and disappears. And the other..."

"The other what?" asked Bertha sharply, raising her chin. Ivy huddled back behind Granny's legs.

"We all know what it is that you do, Bertha."

"What's it to you?" Bertha flipped her red hair defiantly. "At least, I'm in a better trade than my sister – assuming she got pregnant the way that I think she did."

"Stealing is hardly any better," snapped Granny.

Bertha looked away, going quiet. Ivy glanced up at her; she was gazing down the street, her eyes filled with tears. She stared into the distance for a few long, silent moments before turning back to Granny. Ivy shrank back. "I didn't come here today to argue with you," she said coldly.

"No, I suppose you didn't." Granny sighed. "I've done my bit of cleaning up your sister's mess. Now it's your turn."

"How can you talk like that in front of her?" Bertha shook her head. Then she knelt down, and Ivy found herself suddenly on eye level with this aunt she'd never met. She stepped back, but something about Bertha's eyes captured her. They were the same shade of green as Granny's, but that was where the similarity ended. Instead of being cold and staring, Bertha's eyes glittered. She had freckles across her nose and cheeks, and one corner of her mouth was quirked up just a little, as if she was about to burst into laughter at any minute. The expression soothed something inside Ivy, and she stood quietly, looking mutely back at her aunt.

"Hello there, love," Bertha said softly. "You look just like your mama."

Overcome by shyness, Ivy said nothing. She just gazed at

Bertha, feeling a flutter of something that could have been hope.

"You've got her pretty blue eyes, don't you?" Bertha murmured. "Although your mama had something of a hook nose. You must've gotten that pretty little button nose from your papa, whoever he was."

Ivy nodded, knowing that this was about the only safe response when any of the adults in her life spoke to her. Bertha slowly held out a hand. Ivy shrank back but didn't flee.

"Come on, darling," said Bertha softly. "Why don't you come here with me?"

Instinctively, Ivy gripped her grandmother's dress again, retreating closer to Granny. She shook her head, but Bertha didn't try to grab for her. Instead, she just smiled, keeping her hand held out.

"I know change is frightening," she said, "but I promise you and I will have fun together. We'll play every game you can think of, and we'll look up at the stars, and we'll explore all over this London town, we will."

The stars. Ivy had glimpsed them once or twice, but normally she was cuddled on her blanket in the corner long before they came out. She took a little step closer. "Games?" she whispered.

"Yes, my sweet. We'll play twenty questions, and tag, and plenty of other special games that I'll teach you."

Ivy hung her head. "I don't know any games," she murmured.

"That's all right. I'll teach you," said Bertha. "And I'll tell you stories, and show you how to read, just like your mama used to."

Ivy stared at her. "Can you tell me stories about my mama?"

Suddenly, Bertha's eyes filled with tears. She held out both arms, nodding, as a tear coursed down her freckled cheek. "Yes, love," she said. "I'll tell you all about your mama."

It was all Ivy needed to hear. She ran forward, straight into Bertha's safe, warm arms.

CHAPTER 2

The manor floor was made of a dark wood so smoothly varnished and diligently polished that Ivy could see her reflection in it as she worked the brush to and fro across it, clutching the coarse wooden handle in both of her small hands. Soap suds slithered across the floor, dampening the knees of Ivy's ragged little dress, but she wasn't paying much attention to them. Instead, she kept one eye on Bertha, who was mopping the floor a little way across the room. Ivy's job was supposed to be to scrub at any stubborn stains that Bertha's mop missed, but she knew that she had another job, too. The scrubbing was only pretend, Bertha had said.

Across the room, Bertha noticed Ivy looking at her. She appeared strange in her housemaid's uniform, her hair neatly tied back in a headscarf. As Ivy stared at her, Bertha gave her a little wink. Trying her best not to giggle, Ivy winked back, then turned back to scrubbing at the floor. She knew Bertha would give her a cue soon.

The door to the study opened. Ivy didn't look up, listening to the master's heavy footsteps as he walked inside. She heard him rummaging among the things on his desk; she heard his grunt of dissatisfaction. A drawer slammed, then a desk door.

"You there." Ivy glanced up, but the master was addressing Bertha; he was tall and intimidating with his curling white mustache. "I could swear I had taken my pocket-watch with me, but it's not in any of my pockets. Where is it?"

"I couldn't say, sir," simpered Bertha with a pretty curtsy. "Don't you usually put it away in the little safe?" It was mounted on the wall directly beside her; she gave it a friendly little pat.

"Hmm." The master gave Bertha a sharp look, then walked toward it. She took a step out of the way. He took a shiny brass key-ring out of his pocket and unlocked it. As the door opened, Bertha said, "I'm sure I saw you putting it in there, sir."

That sentence – that was it. Ivy's cue. She almost fell over herself in her hurry. Grabbing the bucket of soapy water beside her, she moved it across the floor, then let go of its metal handle while it was standing straight up. It fell back against the bucket with a deafening clang.

It worked. The master jumped, spinning around. "What in the blazes was that?" he shouted.

Ivy cowered. "I'm – I'm so sorry, sir." She gasped. "It – it just slipped through my fingers. It's so soapy."

"You'll give me heart failure, you stupid child," the master roared. "What is my housekeeper thinking, employing a toddler like you?"

"So sorry, sir." Ivy hung her head, but as her blonde hair fell over her face, she peered up between its strands at Bertha. While the master's back was turned, her aunt's hands moved with devastating and invisible speed. Something golden disappeared into Bertha's apron pocket; a moment later, the pocket-watch was balanced on top of a pile of papers inside the safe.

Still shaking his head and muttering, the master turned back to the safe. By then, Bertha was standing helpfully beside her mop, peering over his shoulder. "Sorry about the little girl, sir," she said. "She can be quite clumsy sometimes. But I do think your watch is in there, sir."

"Here it is." The master grabbed the watch, stuffing it unceremoniously into his pocket. "Do something about that child," he added and swept out of the room.

Ivy waited until he was safely out of earshot before grinning and running up to her aunt. "It worked, Auntie!" she cried.

Bertha laughed. "Of course, it worked, my little pumpkin," she said. "Don't your auntie's ideas always work?"

Ivy giggled in delight, clapping her hands. "They always work," she chanted. "They always, always work!" She grabbed Bertha's hands. "Can I see it?"

"Oh, all right." Bertha pulled her apron pocket open. "Just a peep."

Ivy peered into the depths of the pocket. There were bits of thread and small bars of soap in there, and among it all, the gentle gleam of a thin golden chain. "It's so pretty," she breathed. "What are we going to do with it?" She glanced down at her rags. "Can I have a new dress, auntie?"

"Of course, you can, chicken." Bertha tapped her under the chin with a finger. "Anything for you. Now come on – let's get back to work before someone gets suspicious."

❦

THE GOLD CHAIN GLIMMERED IN IVY'S HANDS. SHE allowed it to trickle through her fingers, its tiny links as soft as silk, yet hard and tough when she squeezed them in her fists. She lay flat on her back on her narrow pallet, holding the chain up to the tiny wisps of grubby sunlight that made their way into the servants' quarters through the little window set high in the top of the wall. Looking out of the window was useless, she knew; all she'd see was feet and cart wheels going by on the street above. But down here, gold glimmered.

"When are we going to get my new dress, Auntie?" asked Ivy.

"It's going to be a little while yet," said Bertha, who sat on her own little bed pushed up against the opposite wall of the narrow room. She brushed back a frizzy lock of hair, focusing on darning one of Ivy's socks. "Not until next Sunday afternoon when we've got some time off again."

Ivy giggled. "I like playing these games with you, Auntie." She frowned. "But why do I have to call you mama when we're at work? And why do you call me Gertie?"

"Like I told you, darling, it's all part of our game," said Bertha. Her smile was as warm as the color of her hair. "We just have to play it together for a little while. It's just pretend."

"The master doesn't know we're playing a game, though," said Ivy. "He thinks we're just lying, doesn't he?"

Bertha put down the sock and studied Ivy, her green eyes curious. "What's making you talk like this, love?" she asked. "You're only four years old. How come you're thinking of this kind of thing?"

Ivy looked away. "Sorry, auntie."

"No, honey, don't be sorry." Bertha got up and came over to Ivy, kneeling on the floor beside the pallet. "Tell me what's going on in that empty little head of yours." She gave it a friendly tap with her finger. "Two years you've been with me, and you've never asked these kinds of questions before."

"Well, I overheard the masters' children when they were in their lessons," Ivy confessed. "I was busy dusting their room, and their governess was telling them about how it's wrong to say things that aren't true. She said it was lying, and that the children would be in very big trouble if they were ever caught."

"Ah, I see." Bertha smiled. "Well, Ivy, I suppose the governess isn't wrong. We *would* be in very big trouble if the master ever found out that I was your auntie Bertha Harris instead of your mama, Cordelia Thompson. But do you know what we do when we get into very big trouble?"

Ivy grinned, clutching the gold chain tighter, and nodded her head.

"What do we do?" asked Bertha, tickling Ivy's sides. "What do we do, my sly little darling?"

Ivy squirmed, laughing. "We run away!" she giggled breathlessly. "We run away!"

"Yes, we do indeed." Bertha gave her a fond peck on the top of her head. "And then we find a new game, and we have just as much fun, don't we?"

"We do." Ivy clutched Bertha's hand. "I love you, Auntie Bertha."

"I love you too, little one." Bertha smiled, brushing Ivy's hair out of her face with a gentle hand. "Now pass me that pretty shiny chain, and off you go to dreamland, all right?"

"All right." Ivy handed over the chain and pulled the covers up to her chin. "Will you sing to me, auntie?"

"Anytime." Bertha sat down on the floor, laying one hand on Ivy's tummy. Ivy closed her eyes, allowing the warmth and sweetness of her aunt's voice to wash over her. *Quiet little baby, I sing anew. Auntie's got riches to give to you...*

And long before Bertha could sing about the diamond ring, Ivy was fast asleep.

⚜

GRANNY HAD IVY BY THE HAND. SHE SCREAMED AND fought, punching and pinching at the cruel fist that had closed harshly over her small fingers, but to no avail; it was as if the old lady's hand was suddenly made of iron. Ivy felt herself being dragged over the floor as Granny marched relentlessly on.

"Let me go!" she screamed. "Let me go!"

But she knew what was happening. She was going to be dragged to the fire, because she'd been a bad girl. And Granny would get one of the pokers and hit her with it. Ivy screamed again, fighting with all her strength. If only Granny would let go of her hand—

"No! Granny!" Ivy sat up with a yelp. Her skin was covered in sweat.

"Hush! Hush, sweetheart. You need to be quiet now."

Ivy's heart thundered in her ears as she looked around wildly. But there was no fire here, no pokers, and no Granny. She relaxed, realizing that the hand gripping hers wasn't Granny's unforgiving fist, but Bertha's.

"I'm sorry, Auntie," she whispered. "It was a dream. Did I wake you?"

"Shhh." Bertha laid a finger on Ivy's lips. Her eyes were dancing. "No, you didn't wake me, love – but somebody did. It seems like the master found out about our little game." She winked. "It's time to go and play a new one."

Ivy rubbed her eyes, sleepily pulling back her blankets. "Did he call the police?" she mumbled, pulling her jersey over her head.

"Indeed, he did. You know this game well," said Bertha with a soft laugh. "Now come on, love – it's time for us to get out of here."

Ivy had made enough nocturnal escapes to know how they went. In a flash, she and Bertha had rolled up their blankets, stowed the gold chain down the front of Bertha's blouse, and stuffed all of their possessions into a single cloth bag. Clutching Bertha's hand, Ivy tiptoed after her on her newly-darned socks, holding her shoes in her spare hand to stay as quiet as possible. The house was silent and dark down in the servants' quarters; Ivy knew from experience that it wouldn't be that way for very long.

They had reached the servants' exit. Bertha opened the door slowly, and Ivy stayed well back against the wall as Bertha checked outside. "All clear," she whispered. "Put your shoes on."

Ivy quickly slipped into her shoes as Bertha hoisted the cloth bag on her shoulder. "Can't we take the pony, auntie?" she asked, giving a longing glance toward the stables.

"I'm afraid not, love. We've got our own feet for running," said Bertha with a laugh.

Suddenly, from the street to their right, there was a tremendous clatter. The swinging light of lanterns filled the street; Ivy heard horseshoes slamming on the cobblestones, the voices of shouting men filling the darkness.

"They're here!" she gasped, grabbing Bertha's hand.

"Over there!" yelled a masculine voice. "In the stable yard!"

"Run, Ivy!" shouted Bertha.

Ivy didn't need to be told twice. Clinging to her aunt for dear life, she began to run as fast as her short legs would carry her. Bertha was faster, and she clung on to Ivy, half dragging her along behind as they fled down the street. Lantern light pursued them, horses snorting as they accelerated behind them.

"We're not going to make it!" Ivy gasped in panic. "We got to turn here! Down this alley!"

"Not yet," panted Bertha. "Be brave, honey. Be brave!"

Ivy glanced back. The horsemen were mere yards behind them, sparks flying from the horses' feet, steam bursting from their nostrils.

"I'm scared," she gasped.

"You don't have to be," Bertha said, squeezing her hand tighter. "I'm right here."

Her words gave Ivy the reassurance she needed to put on a burst of speed. But it wasn't enough. She knew that there was no way it could be enough, not with the horses so close behind them. Ivy's heart was in her mouth as she clung to her aunt. Could Bertha get them out of this one?

"Get ready to duck when I tell you!" Bertha shouted.

The shouts behind them became triumphant. Ivy knew they should have ducked already; she didn't dare look back, her head and eyes straining forward, arms swinging hard with every stride, her feet sliding in her too-big shoes. The horses were upon them. She felt a puff of hot breath in the back of her neck—

"NOW!" shouted Bertha, throwing herself to the left.

Ivy dived after her, half-dragged, half-jumping. They plunged into an alley, both slamming down onto the dirt. Boxes splintered as they fell over them, a stray cat yowled, and rats skittered in the darkness. Ivy rolled over and sat up, looking back at their pursuers just in time to see the horse in front scrambling as its rider leaned back, hauling on the reins to stop. The horse behind it was not so obedient. Its feet beat a rhythmic staccato on the cobblestones for an instant, then it crashed into the horse in front. In a messy pile of limbs and shouting, horses, and men tumbled to an ungainly halt.

Bertha laughed. "Come on, love!" She grabbed Ivy's hand again. "Let's get out of here!"

"We made it, auntie!" Ivy gasped as they hurried off into the shadows, ignoring the angry shouting behind them.

"It was amazing because you were brave." Bertha squeezed Ivy's hand. "The bravest child in the whole wide world – and don't you ever forget that."

Ivy looked up at Bertha's face, only the outline of it visible in the moonlight, a few wisps of hair frizzing madly, painted silver in the light. Nobody had a better auntie in the whole wide world, she decided – nobody at all.

CHAPTER 3

Two Years Later

IVY'S LIPS MOVED SOUNDLESSLY AS SHE GAZED DOWN AT THE word on the dirty scrap of newspaper. The paper was soggy and stained now, very different from the crisp new papers she saw in the arms of paper-sellers on the street corners, but she didn't care about that. All she cared about right now was the single word on the paper in front of her. She traced her finger from letter to letter underneath it, sounding out each one slowly.

"P…" she began. "P… uh…"

"Keep going, love." Bertha wriggled her knee, bouncing Ivy up and down. "Keep on trying. You're doing well."

"Puh," Ivy pronounced slowly. "Puh... R... Pur?"

"That's it! That's the first part. Keep reading," Bertha encouraged.

"Purs... Pursuh..."

"Yes, that's it. You can do this, Ivy. It's a long word, but you can read it."

Ivy nodded. She knew she could; she could do anything if Bertha was helping her. "Pursuh... I? Pursuey... Pursueyt?" She paused, biting her lip. It didn't sound right. "Pursuit?"

"Pursuit! That's it!" Bertha laughed in delight, giving Ivy a hug and kissing her on the cheek. "I can hardly read that word myself, and you just spat it out like it was nothing, didn't you? You're just the cleverest little girl that ever lived, I swear."

Ivy grinned, feeling on top of the world. "Pursuit!" she said. "Pursuit!"

With the noisy street bustling past at the mouth of the alley where she and Bertha were sitting with their scrap of dirty newspaper, Ivy's piping voice attracted little attention. Only a couple of pigeons sitting on top of the wall opposite them turned their heads toward them, cooing and studying them with their slightly crazed, popping-out eyes. Ivy giggled in delight, shaking the paper. "I read a whole sentence, Bertha," she said.

"Read it again," Bertha encouraged.

Ivy cleared her throat. She knew the words now, so it was easier to get through the sentence. "They were ar... ar-rest... ar-rest-ed after a short pursuit," she read.

"That's brilliant." Bertha laughed. "You're the brightest little button, aren't you?"

Ivy grinned. "Thank you for teaching me my letters, Auntie," she said formally.

"Well, it's not the education you deserve, darling," she said softly, "but it's all that I have to give you." She touched Ivy's nose, smiling softly. "Soon you'll be reading whole books, won't you?"

"Whole books?" Ivy shook her head. "Aren't they even longer than newspapers?"

"Yes, they are, poppet."

"But that sounds too hard. I'll never be able to do that."

"Ivy, my darling." Bertha smoothed Ivy's hair back from her face. "You're able to do anything at all that you put your mind to. Do you understand that? Anything at all."

Ivy considered this for a moment. "Even read a really thick book?" she asked. "Like that one that the old master had on his bedside table?"

"Even like that one, darling," said Bertha, laughing.

"Wow." Ivy nodded. "I want to do that. Let's read another sentence."

"Not right now, love." Bertha's eye had wandered into the street, and Ivy saw a mischievous sparkle come into it. "I think we've got something else to do quickly."

Ivy followed her aunt's gaze. There were two men walking side-by-side down the street, chatting pleasantly with one another. Their faces were ruddy and freckled; their bright eyes looked as though they usually gazed out across long distances, and their long strides seemed unsuited for the dirty pavement.

"What do you see, love?" asked Bertha.

"Two men from the country, Auntie."

Bertha grinned. "How can you tell?"

"Their clothes, and the way they walk – just everything. They look nice," said Ivy.

"They do, don't they?" Bertha said. "So what do you think they're just perfect for?"

"The cart trick?" suggested Ivy.

"Exactly." said Bertha. "Come on, my clever girl. They look like easy pickings for the cart trick. You know what to do – off you go."

A few seconds later, hiding in position in the gutter, Ivy

waited for a cart to go by more quickly than usual. Then, she threw herself out onto the street, clutching her leg. Taking a deep breath, she let out the most blood-curdling scream she could – and she'd had plenty of practice.

"Aaaah!" Ivy screamed at the top of her lungs, her shriek reverberating around the narrow street. "My leg! MY LEG!"

She continued shrieking for a few seconds, grasping madly at her left knee. Pausing for breath, she heard running footsteps coming toward her. It was all she could do not to smile. Bertha's favorite trick was working – it always did.

"Help!" she screamed. "HELP ME!"

"Hush now." A soft voice, with a round accent that could only come from the country, spoke near her. A pair of strong hands gripped her shoulders, their touch steady and soothing. "Hush, little one. You'll be all right."

Ivy sobbed, tears coursing down her cheeks. She'd learned how to make them come years ago. "My leg," she moaned. "Oh, my leg."

The other man was kneeling beside her now, his big hands reaching for her knee. "What happened, little missy?" he asked.

Ivy peered through the messy hair that hung over her face. She yelped and yanked her leg away from the man, all the while watching as Bertha made her move. Her aunt was slipping across the street, quick and quiet as a ghost.

"The cart," she moaned, trying again to pull away from the man. "The cart ran over me."

"Ah, no. You poor wee thing," murmured the man.

"It must be broken," Ivy whimpered. "It's broken off, I know it. I just know it!" A fresh round of sobs bubbled up her throat, and she cried as hard as she could, keeping one eye half open to watch. A crowd was gathering around her, and Bertha slipped from one person to the other; Ivy saw coins flash in her hand, then disappear into her pocket.

"Now, now, I don't think it's all that bad, love," said the country man, gently prying Ivy's fingers off her leg. "You'll be all right, you'll see."

Bertha leaned nearer. Her hand went to the man's coat pocket, and Ivy gave another howl of agony to distract him. But this time, it wasn't quite enough. The man flew to his feet, grabbing for Bertha, but stumbled and missed.

"THIEF!" he shouted, the voice that had been so soft suddenly loud and thunderous. It was so frightening that it spooked Ivy's tears clean away. "PICK-POCKET!"

"Run, Ivy!" shouted Bertha, turning tail and disappearing into the crowd.

Ivy didn't need to be told twice. She flew up, diving between the man's legs, and shot forward. His bellow of rage was as loud as a bull's, and the jolt of terror it inspired in Ivy spurred her on. She pumped her arms and legs as hard as she could, ducking underneath lady's skirts, clambering over carts, darting between horses' legs as she heard the man's ponderous footsteps giving chase behind her.

He didn't stand a chance against her speed and agility. In the shake of a lamb's tail, Ivy was over a wall, through a window, and running quietly across the floor of an abandoned house. She heard the man's angry voice go past as he took off down the street outside the front door, chasing nothing but the wind.

Bertha was waiting for her in a corner of the empty room where they'd been staying. She kept a finger to her lips, her eyes dancing as she fixed them on Ivy. When the sounds of the pursuit had faded into the distance, Bertha got up and hurried over to Ivy, grabbing her in a hug. "That was perfect!"

"Was it?" said Ivy uncertainly.

"Of course, it was, love," said Bertha.

"But we had to run away again," said Ivy plaintively. "Why do we always have to run away?"

Bertha laughed. "It's all part of the fun," she said. "Besides – look at this." She reached into her pocket and pulled out two watches and a wallet bulging with coins. "It's enough to keep us for a month."

Ivy laughed in delight, reaching out to touch the watches. "So, we can sleep in an inn tonight?"

"We can sleep in an inn for a week, my darling." Bertha picked Ivy up and twirled her around until she was dizzy and giggling. "I told you that you can do anything you want if you put your mind to it."

Ivy giggled. "Can we read again now?"

"Yes, love. We can read all you want."

They settled down on the floor with the piece of newspaper again, and Ivy plunged herself into the world of the written word. After all, Bertha had said that she could read big books one day – and Ivy believed her.

❧❦❧

IVY LEANED OVER THE PUDDLE, WATCHING HER REFLECTION calculatingly as she ran a hand through her brown hair. They had successfully cleaned out a gentleman's well-padded pockets the week before using Bertha's smelly-beggar trick, and Ivy had been able to wash her hair with real soap. Now, though, it looked much too clean. She ruffled it this way and that, trying to get it to look suitably disheveled, like she'd spent the night on the street instead of inside the inn just behind her.

At last, she got it mostly right: a little scruffy, but not overly so. Then she moved out of the alleyway and walked into the street.

She spotted her target almost immediately. A tall, distinguished-looking gentleman, he sat on the edge of the fountain in the middle of the crossing, reading a newspaper. She glanced down at the rolled-up paper in her own small hands, checking that it was the same one. Then, confidently, she wandered across the street toward him.

He didn't look up as she approached. "Excuse me, sir?" she said, pitching her voice a little bit higher than it actually was. "I'm so sorry to be a bother."

The gentleman looked up. Ivy braced herself, ready to run, but the eyes behind the little half-moon spectacles were friendly. "What can I do for you, little miss?" he asked, obviously charmed.

Ivy cocked her head slightly to the side and put on her most winning shy smile. "Sir, I'm just a little poor girl," she said pitifully, "but I'm trying to get an eddycashun and improve myself." She swallowed. "My auntie says that if I can learn to read, I can go up in the world, so she says."

The gentleman nodded. "Your auntie is quite right, my dear."

"Only trouble is, she's not so good at reading herself." Ivy shyly held out the paper, blinking so that her eyes looked bigger and more solemn. "Neither of us can read this word. Will you help me?"

"I'd be delighted." The gentleman smiled. "Sit down here with me."

Ivy perched on the edge of the wall and glanced over at the

inn. Bertha was watching her from the second-floor window of their room; she gave her a nod when she saw Ivy looking at her.

"It's here, sir," said Ivy, pointing to the article she'd been trying to read.

"Ah, I see," said the gentleman. "And which word is it that you were having trouble with?"

Slowly, the gentleman walked Ivy through the entire article. Ivy kept her charm turned up, just in case, but she found herself thinking that the gentleman would have helped her anyway. When they finished the article, she bounced off the fountain and grinned at him. "Thank you, sir!"

"It's my pleasure, little one." The gentleman gave her a fond look, his eyes dwelling on her bare feet and messy hair. "Here." He reached for his wallet, took out a few pennies, and pressed them into her hand. "Never stop reading, all right?"

"I'll never stop, sir," said Ivy truthfully. "Thank you."

She scampered out of sight back into the alleyway. Making sure that the gentleman was fully absorbed in his own paper once again, she slipped around to the servants' entrance, sneaked in through the kitchen and made her way back to their room. Bertha was waiting for her by the window.

"Auntie," said Ivy, excitedly bouncing into the room. "He helped me read it – the whole thing. We read it all."

"I knew you could," laughed Bertha. She patted Ivy on the head. "I'm glad they help you read sometimes, love."

"And he gave me coins, too," said Ivy, dutifully handing them over.

Bertha's expression softened. "You don't have to ask for coins every time, love. This is about helping you to read."

"But I never asked, Auntie," Ivy protested.

Bertha knelt down, touching Ivy's cheek. "You and Auntie Bertha have a good time together, don't we?"

"Yes, we do," said Ivy. "We have so much fun."

"We do." Bertha sighed. "But one day I want a better life for you than this one. You know that, right, poppet?"

Ivy nodded mutely. She nodded because that was what Bertha wanted her to do, but she didn't understand how anyone could have a better life than the long string of adventures that they had together. Bertha was everything to her. What could be better than spending all day playing together?

"And the key to that is this reading of yours. If you can read and write well, you're already much better off than I am." Bertha kissed her forehead.

"Did I do wrong getting the coins?" asked Ivy quietly.

"No, darling. Not at all!" Bertha laughed, jingling the coins in her hand. "In fact, I know just what we're going to do with them."

Ivy bounced in place. "What are we going to do?"

"We're going to go down to find the innkeeper," said Bertha, taking Ivy's hand, "and we're going to buy as much bread and butter pudding as we can – and eat it all up in one sitting."

Ivy skipped down the stairs after her aunt. She knew that in a few days they could be on the streets again, but for today, there was bread and butter pudding, and reading, and Bertha.

CHAPTER 4

The day of the bread and butter pudding felt like a long time ago and a long way away now. Ivy sat with her knees drawn up to her chest, trying to keep her toes out of the oily puddle that was forming in the middle of the alleyway. Bertha had bundled her up in their single, ragged blanket – filched from the bed in the inn, which they had been kicked out of weeks ago – on the single patch of dry ground in the alley. Now, Ivy was watching the patch shrink as rain continued to pour down, dripping from the eaves and hissing down the gutters in a cold, wet deluge of dreariness.

She was trying to keep herself amused by reading the scrap of old newspaper that had fallen into the puddle and been abandoned, but some of the words were torn, others blurred by the rain. She could only make out a few, and it frustrated her.

Eventually, annoyed, she gave up and simply stared into the curtain of rain that masked the mouth of the alley.

A figure emerged from the grayness outside, and Bertha stepped into the alley. She shook her head, flinging her wet hair out of her face. Her lips were blue with cold but still curved in a smile. "Hello there, poppet," she said, crouching down beside Ivy. "Are you all right?"

"I'm fine, Auntie," said Ivy. "Just a bit hungry."

"Then I have good news for you." Bertha took an apple out of the recesses of her coat. "Just managed to pinch it off the back of the cart. That's all I've got for you today, I'm afraid."

"Things will be better tomorrow, when the rain stops," said Ivy.

Bertha nodded, but her smile seemed a little strained. "Yes, they will, darling." She sat down stiffly on the ground beside Ivy, and a low whimper of pain escaped her lips.

"Auntie?" Ivy grabbed her arm, worried. "What's the matter?"

"Oh, don't worry, my love," said Bertha. "It's just my knee – it's been hurting me for a while. But you'll see. Tomorrow, I'll be right as rain."

"As rain?" said Ivy, staring out into the wet world.

Bertha laughed. "Well, maybe not quite as rain," she said, her tone gentle. "I'm going to have a little sleep, all right, love? Wake me if you need anything."

Ivy said nothing as Bertha pulled her coat up to her cheeks, leaned against the brick wall behind them and closed her eyes. She waited until her aunt's deep breathing turned into a low snore before slipping out of the alley, her feet splashing on the wet street as she headed toward the marketplace. She knew just what she had to do to cheer Bertha up.

The newspaper seller on the corner had his coat collar turned up so far, and his hat pulled down so low, that he didn't even notice when Ivy slipped a paper out of his arms after distracting him with a thrown handful of rocks into the street.

She hugged the damp, but fresh, newspaper to her chest and slipped into a shop doorway, making sure that he hadn't seen her. Like everyone else, he was too focused on the rain to notice – or to care. Ignoring him, Ivy scanned the street. Rainy days, Bertha always said, were no good for trying to find the good nature in people; all they were thinking about was getting out of the rain, and it was better to pickpocket than to attempt to trick them. But Ivy couldn't pickpocket the knowledge out of someone's head. She was going to have to find someone to ask.

Not spotting any useful targets at first, she glanced at her paper for an article that Bertha would enjoy. There was one about a circus that had come to the city – at the top of the article was a picture of a pretty little dog sitting up on its haunches, wearing a ruffled collar around its neck. That would make her aunt smile, Ivy knew.

Looking up again, she spotted an older woman walking down the street, clutching the hand of a young child. She'd be as likely a target as any. Ivy took a deep breath and hugged the paper closer. There was no need to make herself look more bedraggled now; with her hair hanging in dripping strings around her face, she was aware that she looked quite scruffy enough.

Stepping out into the street, Ivy waited for the woman to get closer. There was something stern in the set of her mouth that made Ivy hesitate, but she just had to get a smile out of Bertha. She had to try.

"Good morning, ma'am." Ivy stepped forward with her winning smile, stretching her eyes wide.

The woman gave her a single, sour glance and then stepped sideways, trying to maneuver around her, but Ivy persisted. She followed her, holding out the paper. "I was wondering if I could bother you for a moment of your time, ma'am."

Cornered, the woman had no choice but to stop. She gripped her child's hand tighter, her eyebrows pulling down into a disapproving glare. "What do you want, girl?" she demanded.

Ivy smiled at the child, who was a few years younger than she was. Then, slowly, she held out the newspaper. "See, ma'am, my auntie isn't well," she began.

The woman stepped back. "I'm not going to give you any money. Get out of my way."

Ivy's heart sank slightly. Truth be told, she had been hoping for a few coppers to get Bertha a hot bite to eat, but she could still succeed in her main mission without them. "No, no, ma'am," she reassured her quickly. "I'm not looking for money. Not at all."

The woman's eyes narrowed, but she didn't move. "What do you want, then?"

"As I was saying, ma'am, my auntie's not well, and I wanted to read her something to cheer her up." She showed her the picture of the dog. "Isn't he just darling? I just know my auntie will feel so much better if I read her something funny like this."

The woman regarded her suspiciously but said nothing.

"Ma'am, I don't know all my letters so well," said Ivy. "If you would maybe just help me with one or two of the words..."

The woman moved with a suddenness that Ivy hadn't been expecting. Her cold, hard hand met Ivy's cheek with an audible slap. Ivy staggered, pain blossoming through her face. There was blood in her mouth as she stepped back, clapping a hand to her cheek, staring up in horror and shock at the woman.

"How dare you," the woman shrieked, her voice as high and unpleasant as a harpy's. "Reading? A street urchin like you?"

Ivy thought for a moment that the woman was going to spit at her. Instead, she yanked her child closer. "Do you think I'm a fool?" she shouted. "Street children like you can't *read*. You're trying to pickpocket me, aren't you?" She looked around wildly. "Help! I'm going to be robbed! Help!"

Ivy stared in disbelief. She clutched the crumpled newspaper in her hand, backing away. "No, ma'am. Please, I—"

It was too late for talking. The door to a nearby shop opened and two young men spilled out. One carried an ugly, stout wooden club.

"Help!" the woman shrieked, pointing at Ivy. "She's a little thief!"

The men didn't ask questions. They just charged at Ivy, and she knew that she had no option but to run. Tucking her head down, she bolted down the street at her best pace, ducking and dodging as she headed back to the alleyway. Her heart hammered in all the wrong places. She had to get Bertha, and they would have to get out of here.

Skidding into the alley, she knew that the men were only a few yards behind her. "Bertha!" she screamed, slipping, landing with one knee in the puddle. "Bertha, help!"

Bertha was awake at once. She sat up, grabbing at Ivy's arms. "What is it, love?"

"I tried to get a lady to read to me, and now they're chasing me," Ivy gasped in panic. "Come on! We've got to run!"

Bertha pulled herself to her feet, but a look of pain crossed her face. She clutched at her knee. Ivy knew there wasn't time for this. She grabbed Bertha's hand and pulled, trying to tow her down the alley. "Come on, Auntie! We've got to run!"

"Shhh!" Bertha yanked Ivy back. She looked around, her red hair whipping, and spotted an empty barrel. "In there!" she ordered, shoving Ivy forward.

Ivy balked. "But—"

"Ivy, darling, you have to trust me." Bertha bodily pushed Ivy into the barrel. "Get in and be quiet!"

Skinny as both of them were, there was barely enough room for them both to crawl into the barrel. Squashed up against her aunt, Ivy could hear her rasping breaths as Bertha tugged some broken cardboard and other bits of junk over the mouth of the barrel.

"Shhh," Bertha whispered, putting a hand on Ivy's cheek. "Be brave now, my love."

Ivy held her breath. She and Bertha had never hidden before; running away had always worked. She was sure that the men pursuing them would be able to hear her heart. It bounced and bumped and echoed in her chest, so loud and unruly that it was frightening her. It was only Bertha's steady hand on her cheek that kept her from leaping to her feet and running away for all she was worth.

There were footsteps outside. Ivy trembled, clinging to Bertha. Rough voices. "I think she went this way."

"No, she's gone on down the street," came another.

"Why would she do that? She knows she can't outrun us."

"Also true." The voice paused. "Should we turn over these barrels and see?"

Ivy squeezed her eyes tight shut. They were going to catch her. She knew it.

There was a soft thump as the man put his hand on the barrel. Then, a grunt of disgust. "Look at all this. We'll catch something rooting through this rubbish."

"Let's see if she went down the street instead," agreed the other.

They walked away, and only when their footsteps had disappeared into the distance, did Ivy breathe out. She clung to Bertha, and sobs began to bubble up her chest, bursting on her lips in floods of tears. Bertha said nothing. She just wrapped her arms tightly around Ivy and kissed her, holding her so close that Ivy knew she would never let go.

PART II

CHAPTER 5

Four Years Later

THE DINNER PARTY WAS IN FULL SWING. WAITING patiently in the corner, Ivy fidgeted. Her freshly starched maid's uniform was scratchy and uncomfortable, but she knew that it was all part of this new game of her aunt's. Besides, the big pockets on the sides and in the apron were about to prove invaluable.

The smells in the room were delicious. Ivy closed her eyes, breathing deeply. While her lunch of bread-and-butter hadn't exactly been sparse, she knew that it would be a long time before she'd have supper, and that when she did, it would probably be boiled vegetables and maybe a piece of nameless meat if she was lucky. Here, delicate dishes of all kinds floated by on waiters' trays. Oysters and sausages, soft white buns and bowls of soup – their mingled smells filled the room and made Ivy's mouth water.

Across the room, she caught Bertha's eye. Even in this richly decorated room, her aunt's fiery red hair was still a beacon, despite the gray streaks that had begun to stain it; locks of it straggled out from beneath her maid's bonnet as she stacked dirty plates and glasses on her tray. The room was filled with men smoking, drinking and talking in little knots, enjoying some appetizers before they would be conducted to the dinner itself, but it was still easy to pick out Bertha. She noticed Ivy looking at her and gave her a barely perceptible wink. Ivy braced herself. It was almost time to act.

Slipping through the crowd in Ivy's direction, Bertha continued to pile the crystal glasses and delicate china onto the tray. If the master or mistress or even the housekeeper had been paying attention, Ivy knew that Bertha would have been in huge trouble already. But none of them were looking up; they were all engrossed in their party. Until...

The tray wobbled. Bertha gave a little gasp of horror, but Ivy saw that her eyes were calculating. A single glass teetered on the top of the pile and then, slowly, it tumbled, the light from the crystal chandelier sparkling from its perfect surface. It crashed to the floor and shattered into a million glittering pieces, scattering all over the floor, bouncing off the polished shoes of the distinguished guests. There were gasps from all around, and for one moment, all eyes were on Bertha.

All eyes except for Ivy's. She was slipping through the crowd, moving with the quick efficiency that she'd been practicing ever since she became part of Bertha's life. Her small hands were perfect for the job she was doing – as quick and nimble as her feet were light and silent on the floor. The gentlemen didn't notice her thin body sliding between them or her little hands slipping into their pockets. Loose change, pocket-watches, even a few wallets – they slipped into her fingers and disappeared into her own pockets almost imperceptibly.

By the time Ivy had done a quick round of pickpocketing and found her place at the back of the room again, the master had shoved his way to the front of the crowd. "What is this?" he thundered. "What are you doing?"

Bertha cowered. "Oh, master, I – I'm so sorry," she whimpered. "I must have tripped."

"Tripped?" thundered the master. "Tripped? You won't get away with this." He took a threatening step toward Bertha, then glanced around at his guests and seemed to think better of it. "Clean up this mess at once. I will deal with you later."

There were murmurs of approval from the guests. Ivy hurried over, grabbing the dustpan and brush that she'd had at the ready behind the door, and quickly swept up the shards. By the time she and Bertha were heading toward the door, the guests had turned back to their party, the little incident forgotten in favor of what was surely witty conversation.

"Did you get anything?" Bertha whispered as she closed the door behind them.

Ivy nodded, pulling her pockets open. "Lots."

Bertha glanced inside and her grin widened. "That's my girl," she said. "That'll set us up real nicely."

Ivy frowned. "But won't the men miss their watches and things, auntie?"

Bertha laid a hand on Ivy's shoulder, her expression tender. "They will eventually, my lovely. But did you see all the gilded carriages they arrived in? They'll replace their things before they even really miss them. See, darling, for those men, these watches are just trinkets. But for us, they're food and shelter." She squeezed Ivy's shoulder. "Do you understand?"

"I do," said Ivy, although she didn't. Not really. Even with her aunt's explanation, it was stealing.

"I'm not saying that stealing's a good thing," said Bertha, "but eating's a good thing, and if we want to keep eating, we keep stealing." She winked. "Besides, you've got a natural talent for it, darling. Enjoy it."

She laughed, and Ivy couldn't help joining in her soft mirth. Bertha had to be right – she was always right.

From inside, there was a sudden murmur of voices. Bertha looked up, wariness creeping into her eyes. Ivy listened. The voices weren't laughing – instead, they were rising, and she could detect a note of indignation in them. Then, there was a shout that made them both jump.

"HEY!" it came, loud and masculine. "Where are those two maids?"

Bertha grabbed Ivy's hand. "Time to run."

They pounded down the passage. Ivy's heart raced; her scrawny legs reached and flew, and in a few strides, she was dragging Bertha behind her. There was a crash from behind them and golden light spilled into the corridor as the men rushed from the dining hall.

"There they go!" yelled a voice.

"Stop them!" came another.

Feet rushed after them, but Bertha had an escape route planned. Ivy followed her as her feet carried her unerringly toward the front door. She wondered for a second why they were making a direct dash for it when Bertha's usual tactic was to lead the men on a wild goose chase up and down the house for a while first, but there wasn't time to ask questions. Ivy just clung to Bertha's hand and took the stairs down to the entry hall two at a time.

The men were onto them. As they reached the shiny floor of the hall, the front door invitingly right in front of them, side doors burst open and men poured into the room. Ivy didn't remember there being this many men back in the dining hall, but now there seemed to be hundreds, all flooding into the room, shouting and waving their arms.

"Bertha!" Ivy gasped, terrified.

"Run, girl. Just run!" Bertha ordered.

Ivy redoubled her pace. She knew she was almost towing her aunt behind her now, stumbling and panting, but she didn't have a choice. Her feet slithered on the smooth floor. They had almost reached the doorway, and Ivy prayed that the guards at the front gate had not yet made it to the door.

She seized the great knob and pulled with all of her strength. Bertha helped, and the great door shifted open just a crack. A crack was enough. Squeezing her slender frame through it, dragging Bertha behind, Ivy found herself out in the crisp night air. It snatched at her hair and tore at the bonnet on her head, the starchy collar digging into her throat, as she bounded down the long set of stairs and bolted out across the lawn.

"This way!" Bertha gasped, yanking her toward the hedge. Ivy dove into it, small twigs snapping and whipping at her face. There were a few panting moments of slowness as the hedge grabbed at her, slowing her down. Then she was bursting out, her hands slamming into paving, and the street lay invitingly wide open in front of her. They would run for the horses now, Ivy knew. They should have just enough time to get away.

"No!" Bertha's voice behind her was a strangled gasp of

desperation. Ivy whipped around. Her aunt clung to two of the sturdier branches of the hedge, but she wasn't crawling forward. She was holding on in dismay, her face twisted with pain.

"What is it?" cried Ivy.

"My knee." Bertha shook her head. "Run, darling, run! I'll be right behind you."

But Ivy took one look at Bertha's drawn face, heard the footsteps of the men just behind, and knew it wasn't true. She lurched forward, grabbing Bertha's arm, almost too late. As she yanked Bertha forward, one of the men seized her aunt by the ankle. Bertha gave a yell of pain, and Ivy pulled harder, but her aunt was slipping out of her hands, dragged backward toward the lawn.

"Go, Ivy!" Bertha moaned. "Go!"

"No!" Ivy shouted. "I'm not letting you go!"

She flung herself to the ground, leaning back, bracing her feet against the hedge and pulling, but she knew she would never be able to overcome the man who was pulling Bertha by the ankles. Desperate, not knowing what else to do, Ivy pulled back, plunged her body back into the hole in the hedge, and planted both of her small shoes directly in the man's face. He howled in pain, letting go of Bertha for a moment. It was all Ivy needed. She flipped around and scrambled forward, a handful of Bertha's dress in her hand, and yanked her free of the hedge.

"Ivy—" Bertha gasped.

Ivy looked up. Some of the men had run around to the front of the gate, and they were rushing toward them now. She glanced down at Bertha, her face ashen, and knew that they weren't going to make it. Her eyes fell on a large dark hole, just a few feet away. Unless...

"Come on!" Ivy cried. "Help me!"

Bertha didn't ask questions. Bertha shoved Ivy down first. Terrified, Ivy slithered down the black hole, her hands and arms skidding on the slimy surface. Her feet splashed in water, but it was only ankle deep. She shuffled out of the way as Bertha followed. What was this place? Why would there be a hole. It seemed to be some kind of passage or something.

The darkness was complete. Ivy trembled, hearing rats squeaking somewhere in the darkness.

"Auntie, I'm scared," she whispered, hearing the men's shouts echoing around the tunnel above them.

Bertha's fingers found hers and squeezed them tight. "Be brave, lovely," she said. "Just be brave."

They crept a ways further into the wet darkness and hid there, shivering in the cold and damp. The smell of something dead—some animal—was unbelievable; the way the men's voices echoed above them even worse. Apparently, though, the stench was worse for the men than losing their watches. After a few minutes, their voices receded into silence.

"Auntie?" Ivy whispered.

Bertha wrapped an arm around Ivy's shoulders. "Yes?"

Ivy swallowed. "I don't think we should try to run away anymore."

There was a long silence, and Ivy thought she heard her aunt utter a single, tiny sigh.

"No, darling," said Bertha softly. "I don't think we should, either."

CHAPTER 6

London's streets had never seemed so empty or so cold.

Ivy shivered, pulling her over-sized coat a little tighter around her neck. The wind clutched and dragged at it, and Ivy did her best to keep it closed, but its last button had finally given up. Snowflakes swirled around her legs, and she was sure a few had made their way up the coat and onto her frozen skin. She wondered if she would even be able to feel them if they had – she could swear her skin was just as cold as the snow.

Squinting against the eddies that spun and danced down the pavement, Ivy held out her small hands. Bertha had found gloves for her somewhere, but the thumb of one was missing, and the other had a gaping hole in the palm.

"Alms?" she whispered, her cracked lips stumbling around the word. "Alms for the poor?"

The muffled figures hurrying down the street barely seemed to notice her. A few sidestepped her where she stood on the icy pavement; others crossed to the other side of the street. Only one, so tightly wrapped up in hats and scarves that Ivy couldn't see his face, tossed a single coin in her direction. She dived to catch it, turning it over in her hands. It was a single penny.

Ivy sighed, looking back up. Darkness was rapidly falling, and she knew better than to wander about the streets alone once the sun was gone. She clutched the penny tightly in her hand and hurried back toward the abandoned warehouse that she and Bertha had been calling home for the past few weeks. On her way, she paused at the bakery, and exchanged her penny for a single stale lump of yesterday's bread – at least, she hoped it was only yesterday's. It would fill their stomachs, she hoped, although her own stomach was gnawing at her with a hunger that she doubted an entire banquet would be able to satisfy.

Clutching her coat closed with one hand and hiding the bread inside it with the other, Ivy made her way back down the narrowing streets. Above her, factory smoke belched into the air, its foul stench making its way into her nostrils. There was a faceless, voiceless horde of factory workers moving against her, heading for home. She avoided them as far as she could. She wished she had a home to get back to, even if it was some tenement in a slum somewhere. The clanking of the factories surrounding the old warehouse kept her up at night.

It was shelter, at least, she supposed as she made the last turn and saw the warehouse waiting at the end of the street. Half obscured by the snow, it was an ugly thing; squat and square and unadorned. Its empty windows gaped at her like dead eyes, robbed of their glass and life. Ivy tried not to look at them. Instead of going in through the wide-open main doors – only one of the double doors survived, and it dangled off one hinge, stirring and squeaking in the wind – she hurried around to the side of the building. Climbing on a couple of disused boxes, she slipped in through the window and was swallowed up by the darkness inside.

At least there was no wind in here. Ivy picked her way between discarded barrels and stacks of old rolls of fabric, the remnants of what must have been a textile factory before the fire that had hollowed out most of the second floor. It was toward this floor that she headed now, climbing from pallet to pallet, scrambling over the giant rolls and on the skeletons of the rusting and disused machines. If she stayed high, the others might not see her.

She could see them, however. As Ivy neared the hole in the floor through which she always climbed up to the second floor, she could hear their voices. Firelight flickered up ahead, and Ivy hesitated, the black hole she used as an entrance directly above her head. She glanced up at it. Bertha was waiting, but surely, she wouldn't mind waiting a few more moments. Lying down flat on the top of a high stack of old boxes, Ivy crawled slowly forward until she could peer over the edge of the boxes and into the circle of fire-light below.

She didn't know exactly how many children there were living on the first floor of the warehouse. She didn't care; all she really wanted was to hear the voice of their leader. He was standing at the edge of the circle now, the younger children all clustered around the fire itself. Even some distance from the flames, his hair was so blond it looked like gold, the firelight dancing through it as if every strand had been carefully gilded. It hung almost to his shoulders, and the back was shaggy, as if someone had cut it with a blunt knife.

"... tomorrow's team for singing on the street corner," he was saying. Ivy strained to listen, not caring what he was saying, just wanting to hear his gentle voice. "They didn't do well where they were today. Too many ruffians trying to take the few coins they did get."

"I told you, they need to go to a richer neighborhood." This voice belonged to a sharp-faced girl. Both she and the boy looked a little older than Ivy. "Their purse strings are looser there. And maybe there'll be an unwary gentleman or two whose watch is a little too loose."

"Jane, you know we don't teach the children to steal," said the boy firmly.

"You'd rather have them starve?"

"They won't starve. We've never starved. There's always been enough to get by." The boy's voice was firm, but tender. He laid a hand on Jane's shoulder. "Have faith, Jane. We'll be all right."

Suddenly, the plank of wood that Ivy's left hand was braced against snapped. The pieces of it tumbled down toward the fire, and Ivy saw the boy and girl both whip around. She shrank back, crawling into the shadows as quickly as she could, her heart pounding. She loved the boy's voice, but that didn't mean she trusted him. Their raised voices echoed in the dark behind her as she hurried back to her hole, crawled through it, and ran across the sooty and abandoned second floor.

Where the first floor was packed with junk, the second floor was absolutely bare. Ivy could see the whites of Bertha's eyes gleaming in the darkness even though their hiding place was right at the very back of the gaping room.

"Ivy?" Bertha called.

"Shhh!" Ivy hurried to her aunt, who was leaning against the wall, snugly wrapped in the few holey blankets that Ivy had cut from the leftover fabric lying on the first floor. She knelt beside her, her heart hammering. "The others might have seen me," she whispered.

"Easy, love." Bertha laid a hand on Ivy's hair, her soft eyes searching her. "It's all right. They can't hear us up here, and they'll never find the hole – you stumbled across it quite by accident when we were trying to hide from those fellas we robbed." She smiled. "We're safe up here, tucked away like two little mice in an attic."

"I hope so," said Ivy, relaxing slightly.

Bertha stroked Ivy's hair, even though the movement made Bertha wince. Ivy wondered how many more of Bertha's joints were aching now – she'd stopped complaining weeks ago, and then it had been her hip, her knee, and both ankles. "How was your day, my little mouse? Did you manage to pinch some crumbs from the table?" Her laugh was genuine and bubbling.

"It was all right," said Ivy, a smile coaxed from her by Bertha's infectious laugh. She pulled the slightly squashed bread out of her coat. "Here – eat."

Bertha took the bread and began to tear it in half. Ivy laid a hand on hers. "I've already had my share," she said softly.

Bertha looked up, her eyes searching. A few years ago, Ivy knew she would never have gotten away with the lie. Now, though, Bertha's eyes were cloudy, her pinched and shriveled face more blank than it was shrewd. Her hair was more gray than red. Ivy realized, with a pang of terror, how old her aunt was getting.

"Thanks, love," Bertha said at length, taking the bread. "I'm glad you ate."

Ivy lay down and snuggled against Bertha, listening to her rasping breathing as she ate. And she reflected that perhaps, just sometimes, her aunt had taught her a little too well.

CHAPTER 7

Ivy's black eye stung in the cold. She kept one hand cupped over it, trying to protect it somehow, but her fingers seemed to be frozen themselves. The pain and swelling were a reminder of how badly yesterday's begging had gone. Only a few pennies had found their way into her palm, and not because most of their owners had graciously given them away. She'd been on her way home, clutching the precious coins as tightly as she could, when the group of street children had found her. Unlike the band belonging to the boy with the golden hair, these children were rough and dirty, with foul mouths and shifty eyes that had turned dark with cruel intent when they'd spotted her.

Ivy shuddered, remembering the pummeling that followed. She wanted never to think about it again, but the black and blue bruises on her body wouldn't let her forget.

That was why she was sitting on top of the boxes now, looking down at the open circle that the boy with the golden hair had built for the gang of children he led. She'd managed to learn a few of their names by spying on them. She was too scared to leave the warehouse, even though hunger gnawed at every part of her, even seeping into her hands and turning her legs numb and slow. Moving made her feel like the air was too thick, every stirring of her limbs slow and sluggish.

The children below didn't feel the way she did. They never did, Ivy had learned – although how the boy with the golden hair managed to keep them all fed, she didn't know.

He was busy feeding them now, as she watched. There was a big pot bubbling on the fire in the middle of the circle. Steam rose from the surface of the nameless stew within, and its fragrance reached up to where Ivy hid. Some of the smells were likely a little rotten, but to Ivy's starving senses, they were heavenly. Jane – the girl with the sharp face – was busy stirring the pot, and George stood nearby, holding the hands of two little children who stared at the pot with a familiar hunger in their eyes.

"All right, it's ready," said Jane. She reached out a hand, and immediately a flood of children gathered around the pot, all clamoring loudly for their share. "Stop it!" Jane yelled, but it only seemed to make matters worse. The children pushed and shoved, jostling each other for a place in the line.

"Hey!" The golden-haired boy's pure voice rose above the

FAYE GODWIN

chaos. Immediately, silence fell. The boy's tone was firm but held no trace of anger.

"Get into line, everyone," he said. "There's enough to go around – no need to shove."

Obediently, the children filed into a queue behind the boy and the two little ones whose hands he held. He sent them forward to the fire, and one by one, they mutely held up their crude wooden bowls. Jane shot some of the rowdier children a dirty look, but begrudgingly scooped a spoonful of the stew into each of the waiting bowls.

One of the children, the smallest – a girl who could barely have been older than Ivy was when Bertha had first come to fetch her from her grandmother's house – reached the front of the line with trembling little hands. Ivy hadn't seen her before; she guessed that she was new. With eyes wide, the little girl held up her bowl. Jane spooned some stew into it, and the weight seemed too much for the little girl's arms. The bowl wobbled, then began to tip.

"Oops!" A boy dove forward, catching the bowl and straightening it out. It was too late. A blob of stew slopped out of the bowl and splattered noisily on the filthy floor.

"You little fool!" Jane turned angrily on the child. "Look what you've done!"

Tears welled up in the girl's eyes. "I – I..." she stammered.

"It's all right." The boy shot Jane a stern look. "Don't worry,

60

little one. Jane, it's not necessary to be rude. Peter, Joan, clean up the mess."

Although Jane shook her head disapprovingly, the children scrambled to comply with the boy's orders.

"Please get some more bread for Mabel, Jane," the boy said.

With a sour set to her mouth, Jane turned to where a burlap bag rested on a few pallets. She pulled the mouth of the bag open, and Ivy felt a soft gasp escape her lips. The bag was filled to the brim with food – turnips and carrots, bags of what she presumed to be flour, and even some bread. It was a wonderful stockpile, and it was more food than Ivy had seen in a long time. Even after Jane had closed the bag and turned back to the others, Ivy kept staring at it, and an idea began to form in her mind. It was an idea filled with desperate hope, and it also opened a pit of guilt deep in her stomach.

But it was as Bertha said. Sometimes, one didn't have a choice.

⚜

IT WAS SO COLD, EVEN WITHIN THE OPPRESSIVE WALLS OF the warehouse, that Ivy's breath steamed as she leaned over Bertha. Despite the fact that the sun had to be out by now, it was almost perfectly dark in their little nook. Only a few slanting beams of light from the streetlamp outside made their way through cracks in the wall to illuminate Bertha's sleeping face, and what Ivy saw by that light scared her.

She remembered a time, not so long ago, when her aunt's face had been vibrant and rosy-cheeked, glowing with life; her hair a cascade of red, like a flame burning down her back. Now, her face was little more than a skull, eyes lost in sunken sockets, the cheeks etched in brutal detail by the emaciation that had stolen the attractive curves from Bertha's body.

She looked like she should barely be breathing. Ivy swallowed, touching Bertha's shoulder. "Auntie?"

Bertha's lashes fluttered, and her eyes opened. These, at least, were unchanged; when they settled on Ivy, they were aflame with love.

"Morning," she said, struggling to roll over. Her face twisted with pain, and Ivy grabbed her arm to help her sit up, propping her against the cold wall. "Are you all right, Auntie?"

"I'm fine. Just a little hungry."

Bertha touched her cheek. "Are you going to try pick-pocketing again today?"

"Not today. I've got another idea." Ivy tenderly kissed Bertha on the forehead. "I'll be back soon."

Bertha searched Ivy's eyes. Any other time, Ivy knew, she would have wanted to know every detail, but now even the effort of sitting up seemed to have drained her. She nodded. "Be careful, darling."

Silently, Ivy slipped down the hole and onto the top of the stack of pallets. She listened, but nobody shouted out. Quick and silent as a feral cat, she scampered along the stack, heading this time deeper into the warehouse instead of out toward the window she used to get in. She'd spent all day scouting out her route, and she slipped from pallet to pallet, avoiding each creaky plank and loose nail. By the time her feet hit the warehouse floor, she hadn't made a sound.

She was close now, separated from the circle of light where the other children lived only by a few big rolls of fabric. When they spoke, their voices sounded so close that Ivy dropped to the floor, glancing around in panic.

But they were on the other side of the rolls. "Do you think they'll be all right on their own today?" It was the boy with the golden hair.

"They'll be fine." The voice belonged to Jane, and Ivy's heart sank. Of all the children that could have been left at the warehouse on this particular day, did it really have to be her? "You've taught them what they need to know – and besides, Penny is with them. She's the same age as we are."

"I know." The boy sighed restlessly. "I just feel I should be on the street watching over them instead of sitting here guarding our stockpile."

"Someone has to guard this, George. If we lose our stockpile, what will happen on rainy days when the children don't bring in enough food for everyone?"

"I know. I just—" George sighed. "I worry about them. You know how it is."

"You're catching a cold – you said it yourself. I can hear your stuffy nose. It's better for us all if you stay here for a day rather than getting really sick." Jane's voice softened. "You know we won't survive without you."

Ivy peered between the rolls of fabric. George and Jane were sitting a little distance away from the pallet where the bag of food was lying, facing each other, both leaning against heaps of old junk. George was chewing thoughtfully on an apple core, gnawing it down to the very seeds. He gave Jane a curious look.

"I didn't think I'd hear that again from you, Jane," he said. "You've been so... so..." He sighed again. "I don't know."

Jane looked away. Her expression was hard, but Ivy thought she could see pain in it. "I don't mean to be rebellious, George. I care about you."

George shot her a startled glance. Jane shook her head, trying to hide her blush. "I care about all of us," she said, louder. "And I know you're the best leader we could ever hope for. I just don't agree with everything you do."

George folded his arms. "This is about the stealing, isn't it?"

"We should do it, and you know it." Jane raised her chin. "The children do all right with their begging and singing, but it doesn't compare to the way we could live if we brought in money using... other means."

"No." George shook his head firmly, making his shaggy hair ripple.

"George, please." Jane reached out and touched his arm. "Don't be a fool about this. Look at all those... those *rich* people out on the streets." Her lip curled with disgust. "They've got gold hanging on their wrists! They don't know what hunger is. Not the way that we do. What harm does it do to them to take a little of their excess and use it for getting things we really need to stay alive?"

"Jane." George looked directly into her eyes, and his expression was so serious that it made Ivy's own heart flip. "I don't rescue these little ones off the street in order to help them become common thieves. We're not going to steal. And that's final."

Jane tossed her hair. "How is this hoity-toity high ground of yours so much more important to you than keeping everyone warm and fed?" she almost shouted.

Her raised voice was Ivy's cue, a welcome distraction. They were so focused on their argument, Ivy knew that they wouldn't see her coming – because Bertha had taught her long ago that the best kind of target was two people in a quarrel— one could strip them of their purses or watches before they knew it. She had to act now or never. Tucking in her thin belly with a gasp, she squeezed between two of the fabric rolls and froze at the edge of the circle. A few yards of open space separated her from her goal.

"Life is about more than that, Jane," George returned, his voice rising in anger.

"There won't be a life left for us if we don't do something differently," Jane shot back.

Ivy knew she had to move. She took a deep breath, but hesitated for one moment, a strange, stray thought sweeping through her head. *What will George think of me?* Shame boiled in her gut.

Then she thought of Bertha, her weak chest barely rising where she lay, and a jolt of determination set her feet moving. Quick and silent, she skimmed across the floor, plunged her hands into the welcome abundance of the sack. Her fingers closed on something – something crumbling like bread in one hand, and the fabric of a smaller sack in the other – and she pulled them back quickly. She didn't stop to look down at her prizes. Instead, she spun and ran back toward her hiding place, but she was too quick. There was a loud slap as her right foot met the floor.

George and Jane fell abruptly silent. In the split second that followed, Ivy redoubled her speed. "HEY!" Jane's voice shrieked. "Get back here!"

"Stop!" George commanded.

His golden voice was so loud and pure that Ivy almost did stop. But her momentum carried her forward. Clutching the stolen bounty to her chest, she dove between the rolls.

"Cut her off!" shouted Jane. "Catch her!"

She heard their feet pounding behind her and looked up, toward her little home above. If she gave away their hiding place, what would Jane or the others do to Bertha? Instead, Ivy wheeled toward the broken window, scrambling through the junk, her path loud and erratic now, desperate with the flight of a trapped animal. She heard them shouting, and fear shot through her body. But she was only a little way from the window now. Just to jump on this next set of boxes—

Ivy slipped. Instinctively, she tightened her grip on the food in her hands, and her knees slammed on the harsh floor of the warehouse. Pain blossomed through both knees, but her fear was stronger, and she struggled back to her feet. In two bounds, she was on the windowsill and tumbling out of it into the alley. Her aching knees forced her to dart behind the nearest stack of broken barrels and sit there, trembling, trying not to pant too loudly, as she heard George and Jane reach the window.

"Come on!" Jane shouted. "Give me a leg-up. Let's get after her!"

"No. It's no use." George was breathless; she heard him sniff and wipe his nose before continuing to speak. "We can't leave the food unguarded."

"Then you stay. I'll go after her."

"I said no, Jane. It's no good – she's gone." He sighed. "Don't be too upset. We still have plenty – I saw the bag was still full when we ran past it. Besides, she was just a child, like us. Younger than us by three or four years, I should think." His voice was gentle. "She probably needed it more than we do."

Jane's voice grumbled as they moved back into the warehouse, but it wasn't her harshness that made Ivy sink her chin on her chest and sob, clutching the squashed bread and half-torn bag of vegetables. Nor was it the throb in her knees or the hunger gnawing at her guts or even the thought of Bertha, a shadow of herself, wasting away up in that dank corner of the warehouse.

It was George and his gentleness. And the fact that she'd stolen from him.

CHAPTER 8

Ivy's fingers froze to the icicles so fast that they felt sticky to the touch as she pried them loose from the frigid eaves above the single, tiny window on the whole second floor. At least her fingers had gone numb by now. She dropped the last icicle into the cracked bowl in her free hand and blew on her fingers. They weren't sore, but they were a worrying kind of blue.

Feeling her way back across the darkness of the warehouse, Ivy kept her eyes fixed on the tiny fire she'd built beside her aunt, using bits of the broken boxes and pallets from down below. She knew it was risky, but the night was so cold that she feared freezing more than she did burning to death. Reaching the fire, she used an old bit of damp wood to scrape some of the coals out from beneath it and placed the bowl on top of them. The icicles began to skid around as they melted.

"Ivy?"

Ivy looked up. Bertha's eyes were two glowing points of light and life in a face so gray that it looked as if it might fall to ash at any minute. Ivy remembered a time when they had danced around their tiny fires, laughing and singing about the scraps that they had for supper. Now, though, it seemed to be almost too much effort for Bertha to summon up a smile.

"Sorry, Auntie." Ivy sat down beside her and wrapped her hands around Bertha's cold and bony fingers. "Did I wake you up?"

"It was about time I woke a little," said Bertha. "I've been sleeping all day."

Ivy felt a jolt of fear. She had no idea what that meant. "That must be a good thing, Auntie," she said, trying to force a little optimism into her voice.

"I suppose so, my lamb." Bertha reached up, her hand trembling with effort, and brushed some of Ivy's hair behind her ear. "What are you up to?"

"I just went to get some icicles. I'm making us some soup from the leftovers of that food I pinched for us a few days ago."

Bertha's face slackened into a smile. "I remember," she whispered. "You were so brave."

Ivy felt Bertha's eyes on her as she turned back to the fire and started dropping the scraps of carrot and turnip into the bowl of melted ice. It was a bit murky, but her stomach growled regardless. She couldn't wait until the carrot had gone soft; the fire was dying, and she wanted to fall asleep with just a little light so that the darkness wouldn't feel so big and lonely. After a few minutes, Ivy scratched the last of the embers away, fished their single spoon out from under her makeshift pillow and brought the bowl of slimy soup over to Bertha.

"Here we are, auntie," she said softly. "Let me feed you."

"It's all right, little one." Bertha held up her hand. "You have it. I'm not hungry anymore."

"But Auntie..."

"Now, now, now." Bertha gave Ivy a little wink. "I raised you to respect your elders and betters, didn't I? I told you to eat, Ivy Harris, and eat you will."

There was forced humor in Bertha's tone, but it brought Ivy to tears. Her appetite suddenly ruined, she put the bowl down. "Oh, Auntie," she whispered, and threw herself on Bertha's chest, wrapping her arms around her bony shoulders.

"Hush now, poppet." Bertha stroked her hair. "Shhh. It's all right. It's all right, my lovely. All is well."

"No, it's not," sobbed Ivy. "You're sick. And I don't know what to do." She gasped. "I don't know what's going to happen."

"I do, love." Bertha pressed gently on Ivy's shoulder, pushing her back so that their gazes could lock. Bertha's eyes were runny and red with fever, but the fire and warmth in them was as real as it had always been. "I'm going to die," she said softly.

"Don't say that."

"Shhh." Bertha put a finger to Ivy's lips. "You know I'm right. But it's fine."

"How can you say that?"

"It's just − all right." Bertha smiled. "You know I didn't take you to church all that much, except for that time that we pinched the old lady's mink muffler, remember that? Yes, that was fun, wasn't it, my lovely? But all the same, I learned a thing or two about heaven, so I did. And I know that nobody who spent their lives looking for the light will ever be alone in darkness." She stroked Ivy's cheek. "I certainly never was. Much as I regret it now, I didn't read that much of the Bible, but I do know that one day you and I will be together again. Nothing's stronger than our love, my poppet."

"I know that, Auntie," Ivy whispered, tears running hot and quick down her cheeks. "But what am I going to do without you?"

"You're going to be brave, my love," said Bertha softly. "You're going to be brave." She pulled Ivy close, and Ivy curled up against her aunt, tucking her head into the nook between

Bertha's neck and shoulder. Bertha's voice vibrated through them both as she stroked Ivy's hair, whispering in her ear. "I'm sorry I couldn't take better care of you, my darling. I'm sorry I couldn't do better."

"You did everything, Auntie." Ivy sobbed.

"I tried." Bertha pressed her lips to Ivy's forehead. "One day, my greatest wish for you is that you'll never have to tell another lie again. But until then, you remember what I taught you, all right? And keep looking for the light." Her breaths were quick now, coming in little gasps between her words. "You be brave – you – be – brave – my darling." She took a last deep breath. "You... be... brave."

Then her voice trailed off into deep, slow breaths. Ivy lay with her head on Bertha's chest for a long time, listening to the quick, erratic beat of her heart, until finally sleep stole over them both.

And for Bertha's beaten body, it was the final, merciful sleep that carried her far away from the cruel, cold world.

CHAPTER 9

Ivy had been crying for what could have been hours, or days, or all eternity. She just couldn't stop. She felt that she had cried oceans of tears, that more fluid and grief had poured from her than any human body could possibly have held.

Bertha's hand was cold and stiff in her own. The moment Ivy had woken up that morning and touched Bertha's cheek, she'd known that the body she was curled up against no longer contained the woman that had loved her more than anyone else in the world. As soon as she'd opened her eyes, she'd seen that Bertha – even though she was curled up peacefully on her side, her eyes closed – was gone.

Her head knew it. But her heart couldn't believe that Auntie Bertha, the sun in Ivy's world, had left. It was as if all light had been leached out of the universe. There was nothing else, no bustling street outside, no community of children living down below; nothing but the darkness of the second floor, and the coldness of Bertha's fingers as Ivy clutched them and poured all her sadness into the tears that had been coursing down her cheeks for what felt like forever.

Then, a footstep. Ivy's crying switched off as if a candle had been snuffed out. She whipped around, shrinking back against Bertha's body, even though her aunt couldn't protect her from anything now. The scraps of light that crawled through the gaps in the wall were just enough to illuminate the outline of four figures standing only a few yards away, their shoulders tense, ready to attack.

Ivy didn't know what to do. It was as if her thoughts had all frozen, locked in place by her grief. So she just froze, crouching against the floor like a spooked animal.

"It's her!" The angry voice made Ivy flinch. *Jane*. The name flitted through her emptied mind.

"Who?" piped up a younger voice.

"That girl. The girl who stole our food!" Jane shouted. "Let's grab her!"

"No." This voice soared above the rest, stopping three of the figures in their tracks. It was George. "Look at her. She's terrified."

"I should hope so. She knows she stole from us!"

"Jane." George's voice was stern.

"What's that beside her?" asked one of the younger voices.

"It's a body," said the other, horror filling it. "A dead body."

"Yes, it is," said George gently.

He stepped forward, and the light fell over his face, illuminating his eyes. They were deep brown, and so soft that Ivy felt herself relax a little just looking into them. Pushing some of his messy blond hair back, George took another step nearer, then crouched down. "Hello," he said, very softly. "What's your name?"

Ivy stared at him for a moment that seemed to last forever. What had he just said to her? His question bounced and echoed inside her, but she felt too tired to think about it. The response she gave him came automatically. "Ivy," she whispered.

"That's a pretty name." George gestured at Bertha's body. "Who's that?"

"Bertha." Ivy's voice was a shriveled, shadowy thing. "My auntie."

"I'm sorry. What happened?"

A pause. Ivy looked away, tears filling her eyes and throat. She knew what had happened. Bertha was dead, Bertha had died in the night and she was never, ever coming back. She choked back a sob, and George held out a hand. "Hush. It's all right.

You don't have to say anything." His voice was soothing, and Ivy looked back at him. "Do you have anyone else?" he asked quietly.

Ivy shook her head.

"That's all right. None of us did either." He held his hand out again. "Why don't you come with us?"

"I stole from you," Ivy whispered. She glanced shamefully at the sack, still lying beside the bowl of congealed soup. "I took your food."

"I know," said George, "but you were hungry, and you didn't know any better. We can show you better. Just come with us."

"She can't come with us, George," Jane hissed. "We've barely got enough to go around as it is."

"She'll help us," said George, not taking his kind, steady eyes off Ivy. "I know she will. You can help us get food, can't you, Ivy?"

Ivy nodded.

"Then that's settled. Come on. We've got something for you to eat, and there's plenty of us, so you'll be safe."

Ivy looked back at Bertha, clutching her dead hand even tighter. Her aunt's eyes were closed, and her face looked peaceful. In the past eight years, they'd never spent more than a few hours apart.

"I don't want to leave her," she whispered.

"Ivy, look at me." George's gentle voice compelled her to obey. "She's already left you. She's gone off to a better place."

Jane snorted, but George ignored her. "Now it's up to you to keep going, all right? And you've got to come with us. You'll be safe with us." He paused. "Don't you think that's what Aunt Bertha would have wanted?"

Ivy thought of Bertha's words. *Keep looking for the light.* She looked over at George, and he was the brightest thing she could see. So she reached out and took his hand, and his big, strong fingers curled around hers. A smile tugged at his face. "That's it," he said. "Come on. Let's go."

And step by step, he led her away, leaving the shell of Bertha, alone in the corner of the warehouse in the dark.

CHAPTER 10

"Thomas, Peter, Duncan, you're going to the marketplace today." George was standing at the front of an obedient queue of children, handing out chunks of half-stale bread wrapped in old newspapers. "Joan and Penny didn't have much luck begging there today, so let's try a bit of singing and see if people will be a little more generous for that."

The boys took their bread and hurried off, giggling and jostling one another, singing a few lines here and there as they joked about who could be the better singer. George turned to the handful of children that were left, glancing over them quickly. "Jane, you take Peter and go to the rich houses – they'll have thrown something out that we can use. Gordon, you're coming with me. Timmy, Faye, guard the food. And Penny, you can take Ivy and Joan. Try that crossing with the fountain in it this time – those people generally seem to be in a better mood."

Ivy held out her hands, dumbly receiving her chunk of bread from George. She tucked it into her coat pocket, and for a moment, George's eyes met hers. They were filled with concern.

"Look after her, Penny," George said. "She'll need you."

"How am I supposed to look after both of them?" asked Penny, exasperated, trying to keep hold of the giggling, squirming Joan.

"Just do your best." George smiled. "All right – let's be off. And remember, be back by six o' clock, or we'll be coming to look for you."

Ivy followed Penny's homely figure out of the warehouse. After so many months of slipping through the broken window, it still felt strange to walk out of the big doors, even though Ivy had been staying with George's gang for a few days now.

Her feet followed Penny as they walked down the streets, but her heart was far away, remembering when she and Bertha had walked together. They had been in one of the wealthy areas, working as housekeeper and maid for some rich family, when they'd heard the clatter of hooves behind them. Turning around, Ivy had seen a most splendid sight. Six pitch-black horses came charging down the street, their manes flying, plumes waving, shoes flashing as they lifted their hooves high into the air. Behind them, they drew a black carriage that gleamed in the sun, and it was followed by such a procession of people all in black – many of them wailing loudly in despair – that Ivy's jaw hung open as they passed.

"What was that, Auntie?" she had cried.

Bertha laughed, sweeping Ivy up onto her shoulders. "A funeral procession," she said.

"What's that?"

"It's when an important person dies and they parade their body through the street to let everyone know how important they were," said Bertha. "Basically."

Ivy considered this, winding her fat little fingers into Bertha's vibrant red curls. "When you die, I'm going to have ten black horses pull your carriage," she said. "And lots more crying people to follow you around."

Bertha laughed. "I appreciate that, darling," she said, "but it's not what I want."

"What would you want, then?"

Bertha's voice grew misty. "Flowers," she said softly. "Just lots and lots of flowers."

Flowers. They were walking through one of the shop districts now, and Ivy's eyes lit on a florist's shop. A display of the most beautiful blooms formed a blaze of brilliant color among the grayness of the other shops. They were proudly arranged in the window box, and their colors seemed to light up the world: yellow and purple, shining white, brilliant blue, and a red that burned the way that Bertha's hair used to. Ivy found herself wandering in that direction. She could hear Joan giggling, Penny's running feet and exasperated shouts as she gave chase after the errant little one. It was the perfect time to slip away.

Ivy's hands and feet seemed to move of her own accord. She watched the shopkeeper, her brain filled with cold calculation. When the man looked away, smiling at a customer, Ivy moved fast. She didn't run – running was for afterward. Her steps were brisk, quick, confident as she passed by the window, and her hands were even quicker, scooping flower after flower behind her back. It was only when she started running that they started yelling, and she knew from experience that their yells could not keep up with her running.

She gave them the slip within a few minutes. Barely breathless, she headed back toward the warehouse. It was child's play to sneak past Timmy and Faye where they sat watching the food. She tucked herself back through her hole and made her way toward the corner on the second floor.

Bertha's body looked sunken in somehow. It didn't look like Bertha anymore, except for a few strands of the hair; they were as vibrant as ever, gleaming in the dots of faint sunlight that sparkled on them. Ivy tried not to look at any of the body, or the rats, or anything except that shining hair. One by one, she took the flowers and started to arrange them all around her face and head. She covered up the sunken cheeks and the strange bruising that had appeared along the face where it was pressed against the floor. She left just the eyes, and the hair – the glowing red hair that had been a beacon of light for all of Ivy's life.

Then she sat down, her arms wrapped around her knees, and just stared at the colors of the flowers.

"Ivy?"

Ivy didn't move. She'd barely blinked since sitting down here; now, the air had turned cold outside, and her knees were aching steadily. Still, her eyes remained fixed on the wilting flowers and the shiny strands of her aunt's red hair.

"I thought I'd find you here."

George sat down beside her, so close that she felt the air stir as he moved. Part of her wanted to look up at him, but she couldn't drag her eyes away.

George shifted on the floor, getting comfortable. "How long have you been here?"

There was a long pause. "All day," Ivy whispered. Her voice felt dry and cracked from the silence.

"Where did you get the flowers?"

Ivy didn't answer, but for the first time all day, she really felt something: guilt. She stared at the flowers, and suddenly they didn't seem like such a gift anymore.

"She was special to you, wasn't she?"

"She was everything." It was the only word Ivy could think of to describe what Bertha had been.

"How long had you stayed with her?"

Ivy shrugged. "Since I can remember."

"You're lucky to have had her," said George softly. "Was she kind?"

"Always. And funny and loving." Ivy swallowed. "She always knew how to make me laugh."

"The woman who raised me wasn't my mother either." George's voice was flat, matter-of-fact. "But she wasn't so kind. Still, when she died, it felt like my whole world had ended. Like there was nothing left." He cleared his throat. "Like the sun had gone out."

Ivy nodded, feeling tears prickle behind her eyes. "What did you do?"

"What could I do? I found this warehouse. I found little kids, younger than me, who needed someone. And that became..." He paused. "It became who I am, and my reason for going on." He touched her shoulder, and a bolt of emotion ran through her body. "You've got a reason for going on, too, Ivy.

But until you find it, I need you to never come up here again. I need you to come with me and help me look after the little ones. They need us."

Ivy looked up at George for the first time. Her eyes hurt as they adjusted to the light. "I miss her," she whispered.

"I know you do," said George. "But she's gone. I'm here, though." He smiled. "And so are the others. And we need to work together if we're going to be able to make anything of ourselves." He reached out and brushed some of her hair out of her face. "You've got to be brave now, Ivy."

The words rang like a gong, deep inside her soul. *Be brave*, Bertha had said, time and time again. *Be brave*.

Ivy closed her eyes. "All right," she whispered. "I will."

When George spoke, it startled her. She hadn't been addressing him. "That's it," he said, taking her hand. "Come on, Ivy. Let's go and get some dinner, shall we?"

She followed him out of the second floor, and never went back. Because she didn't leave her aunt up there. Later, she and George carried her body outside. George found a dumpster, and Ivy wept when her aunt's body disappeared inside it.

GIGGLES FILLED THE WAREHOUSE AS JOAN RAN AROUND, HER little bare feet slapping on the floor. Ivy dove to catch her, but the little girl was too quick. She ducked behind one of the sleeping pallets, and Ivy clambered over it, laughing. There was a howl of indignation from Timmy, who currently occupied the pallet, and he threw back his blankets and tackled Ivy. All three children tumbled to the floor in a happy tangle of limbs.

"Got you!" Ivy emerged triumphantly, clutching Joan in her arms. Tired, but still giggling infectiously, Joan put her arms around Ivy's neck. Timmy, grumbling, crawled back into bed as Ivy carried Joan over to the sleeping pallet that the smallest member of their group shared with one of the other little girls. Joan's sleeping mate was already fast asleep. Ivy tucked Joan in beside her, brushing her unruly golden hair out of her face.

"Are you going to sleep peacefully now?" she asked.

Joan pulled her patched and mended blanket up to her chin. "Yes, Ivy."

"That's a good girl." Ivy smiled. "Sweet dreams now."

Joan cuddled up to her friend, pressing her face into the folded fabric that they used for a pillow. Ivy knew she'd be asleep in seconds. She made sure that the blanket was securely tucked around the hard pallet, then straightened up, turning back toward the fire.

George was sitting there, staring into the flames. They reflected brilliantly in his deep brown eyes. He looked up as

Ivy sat down near him, and a smile spread over his features. "Thank you for helping to take care of Joan," he said. "She needs you."

"I..." Ivy looked away. "I think I need her, too."

"We all need each other. There's no shame in that," said George. "That's why we're all together, and why I work so hard to make sure that nobody gets lost or left behind."

"Were you the only one living in this warehouse at first?" asked Ivy.

"No. Gordon and Jane were here when I started to hide here after the woman who raised me died. Jane's my age, but Gordon was still very small. We banded together and found out that we could survive better that way." George shrugged. "It just seemed natural to join others to our group if we found them on the streets."

"Like you found me."

"Something like that." A smile curled the corner of George's lip, and Ivy felt her heart do a little somersault in her chest. Not knowing what to do, she looked around awkwardly, fishing for words, and her eyes rested on a glint of metal on George's arm. His sleeve had ridden up a little, revealing something that gleamed like brass.

"What's that?" Ivy asked curiously.

George glanced down at it. "Oh, this? It's just an armband."

He shrugged. "It's been with me since I can remember – I used to hide it when it was too big. I never told anyone about it, which is odd. But something warned me to keep it secret. When I got bigger, I started to wear it. It got too small for me, but I bent it open. See? I have a feeling it might have belonged to my parents. They must have stolen it from somewhere."

Ivy felt shame heating her cheeks. "I stole all the time," she told George. "The way that I stole the food from you – but not always when I was hungry. Bertha and I pick-pocketed anytime we could, even if we had enough food and somewhere to stay. We had so many tricks that we played on people so that we could steal things from them. We told so many lies so that we could get jobs at fancy houses."

George gave her a quizzical look. "But judging by the way you've talked about her in the months you've been with us, you loved her."

"I did. And she loved me more than anything," said Ivy. "I always knew that. She said it was the only way for us to survive. But we didn't." She swallowed her tears. "At least, she didn't."

"I don't know whether your aunt was right or wrong," said George simply. "I know she meant the world to you. But that's not how our group works. We don't steal or lie."

"We should."

Ivy and George both turned. The irritable voice belonged to Jane. She sat down between them, pushing a wing of her glossy black hair out of her face. Her sharp features were furrowed with annoyance.

"I don't understand why you want to be so stubborn about this," she told George. "You never turn anyone away, but the more mouths we have to feed, the less willing you are to do what it takes to feed them." She shot Ivy a dirty look.

"Stop worrying, Janie." George reached over and touched Jane's shoulder. "We've got enough right now, and there's no need to raise your voice. You'll wake the little ones."

Jane sighed but reluctantly let it go. She scooted closer to George, and he didn't take his hand off her shoulder. Ivy felt a strange new emotion churning in her heart. She didn't know what it was until she looked up into Jane's eyes and realized that it was burning there, too. That was when she saw it for what it was: jealousy.

PART III

CHAPTER 11

Two Years Later

THE EARLY MORNING LIGHT WAS CHILLY IN THE warehouse, and a few snowflakes had blown in through the open windows, swirling around the heaps of junk in lost eddies. Yet what Ivy felt in her heart was filled with warmth. She broke a chunk of bread off the half-stale loaf that she'd taken out of the stockpile bag and held it out to Timmy, smiling. "There you go."

"Thank you, Ivy." The little boy grinned at her, then grabbed Joan's hand. "Come on, Joanie. Let's go!"

"Easy, easy." George laughed, pushing some of his hair out of his eyes. "You don't even know where you're going yet."

"Tell us quickly," said Joanie. "The faster we run, the warmer we'll stay."

"That's the spirit," said George, smiling. Ivy's heart flipped. A few golden hairs had started to dust George's chin and upper lip, and his broadening shoulders made him look a little more like the leader that he was. "It's your turn to do the market-place today," he said, handing the children a few coins. "First stop by the old lady that sells flowers at the side of the road and buy a few. Then see if you've got any luck selling them at a little profit at the marketplace."

"Thank you, George." Joan took the money, and then she and Timmy scampered off. George pulled his holey hat down a little further over his ears. "Penny, Jane, are you ready for a day's begging?" he asked jovially.

"Ready and waiting," said Penny.

"Come on," said Jane. "Let's be off." She had grown much taller over the past few months, but her frame was still just as skele-tal, and her hook nose looked like the beak of a brooding bird of prey as she gathered her coat more closely around herself.

"Wait a moment." Ivy grabbed a chunk of bread and hurried over to George. "You forgot your bread."

George smiled as he took it from her, and their hands brushed together. Ivy gazed up into his deep eyes and felt her heart speed up. His smile only made it pound even faster.

"Thank you, Ivy," he said gently. He reached up, brushing some of her hair back behind her ear. "Will you and Gordon be all right here guarding the food?"

"They'll be fine," snapped Jane. "Let's go, George."

He turned away, and the spell broke. Ivy felt slightly breathless. She clutched the leftover bread in trembling hands as George, Penny, and Jane headed out of the warehouse. "Have a good day!" she called after them.

"You too!" George raised a hand to wave. He stepped outside, the sunlight catching his hair so that it flashed like gold. Ivy kept her eyes trained on him until he was gone.

With a happy sigh, she turned back to the pallets where the food sack rested. Gordon was sitting on the edge of the pallets. Despite his youth, he had dark, knowing eyes, and they watched her warily as she approached. "Isn't it wonderful that George has given us a safe place to stay?" she said, sitting beside him.

"I guess," said Gordon. "I agree with what Jane used to say, though. There are things we could be doing differently."

"Trust me," said Ivy. "Stealing and lying – they're not worth it. It's better to have what we have honestly, even if it's not as much as we want." She smiled. "I'm glad Jane doesn't argue with George so much anymore, and that she realized that what he's saying is true. At first, I thought she really hated him, but now I can see that she only argues with him because she cares about him."

"She does," said Gordon softly. He looked away from Ivy. "And I care about her."

"Of course, you do," said Ivy, slightly taken aback. "You're her brother."

"Yes." Gordon looked up at Ivy, and to her surprise, there was regret in his eyes. "I'm sorry about this."

"Sorry about what?"

Then, the door to the warehouse banged open. Ivy leaped to her feet, grabbing for the sack, ready to run and hide it from whoever had come to take it from them. But when the figure came around the corner of a stack of rubbish, Ivy relaxed, letting go of the sack.

"Oh, Jane!" she said, relieved. "It's only you. You scared me."

Jane's expression was grim. She stopped a few yards from Ivy, her arms folded.

"Is everything all right?" Ivy asked, worried about the look on Jane's face. "What's going on? Did someone get hurt?"

"No," said Jane. "I told George that I wasn't feeling well and came back to the warehouse." She took a step closer to Ivy.

Sweat burst out across Ivy's back and palms. She forced herself not to take a step back. "Are you sick?" she whispered.

"No. I'm here to take care of you." Jane reached out and prodded Ivy in the shoulder with one finger.

"What do you mean?" asked Ivy, aware that her hands were shaking violently.

"You've been nothing but a bad influence since you got here." Jane tossed her head, throwing her hair back out of her eyes. "Your stories about the things you did with your aunt are causing trouble for the younger children, making them want to steal and cheat, too."

"No." Ivy's heart sank. "I'm sorry, Jane. I didn't even know. What did they do?"

"It's not what they did, Ivy." Jane gave her a push this time, and she had to stagger back a few paces. "It's what *you're* doing. You're causing trouble for our entire group. And it's time for you to go."

Ivy swallowed. She planted her feet firmly, crossing her arms. "That's not true. I do my best to help with everything we do."

"That won't change what you are," snapped Jane. "You're a thief and a liar, and you don't belong here."

Ivy wanted to shout that it wasn't true, that she didn't steal or lie anymore. But she was rushed by a flood of memories, of all the things she and Bertha had stolen together. How many purses and pocket-watches had she slipped out of unwitting pockets? How many coins and notes had fallen into her hands because of one of Bertha's schemes?

"We did what we had to do to survive," Ivy whispered.

"And now I'm doing what I have to do for this group to survive." Jane looked across at Gordon and nodded. "Grab her."

"No!" Ivy tried to dodge, but Gordon already had hold of both her arms. She fought and struggled, but Jane lunged closer and grabbed her by the hair. Screaming and squirming, Ivy tried to break free, but their grips were both too strong.

They dragged her into the street, and with a grunt of effort, threw her forward. Ivy's hands and knees slapped down hard on the pavement. Despite the pain shooting through her skin, Ivy scrambled to her feet and turned to face them.

"You can't throw me out!" she cried. "I know where George has gone. I'm going to find him and tell him what you've done!"

Jane lunged close. She grabbed the front of Ivy's jacket, yanking her nearer so that they were nose to nose. Jane's cold eyes burned with rage.

"No, you're not," she warned. "You're never going to go near George again in your life. Because the only thing you've ever done is hurt him. You're a liar, a fraud, and a thief, and he knows it. And it kills him to have you here in his group."

Jane's words were a cold knife thrown straight through Ivy's heart. She thought of how much George hated the idea of stealing in order to survive, yet that was what she had done for eight years of her life. She knew Jane was right. Her very presence was nothing but a torment to George.

Seeing the tears that were filling Ivy's eyes, Jane let go. Ivy staggered back, falling onto her bottom, and stared up at Jane in agony.

"If you really do care for George," Jane said coldly, "there's just one thing you can do to help him."

"Wh-what?" Ivy whispered, dreading the answer.

Jane pointed a trembling finger toward the vast, faceless city that lay out there, waiting to consume anyone who found themselves alone.

"Go," she hissed. "Go away and never, ever come back here again."

For a moment, Ivy wanted to fight, to scream at Jane that she was wrong – that George liked her, too. But she knew the older girl was right. Nothing could ever change the fact that she was nothing but a lowly thief. Tears streaming down her cheeks, Ivy got up, turned around, and began to run.

CHAPTER 12

The falling darkness was terrifying, but it was nothing compared to the cold that came seeping out of the growing twilight. It poked its icy fingers down the nape of Ivy's neck, entwining its insidious hands around her bare fingers, finding its way into her holey shoes. At least now her aching feet were growing steadily numb instead of painful.

Ivy had little idea where she was. She just knew that the rising cold meant one thing: she had to keep moving. Despite the hunger that clawed her stomach and sucked the strength from her bones, she walked through the streets, head low, avoiding the angry stares from the rich people who didn't appreciate the smelly little ragamuffin among them.

Why hadn't she thought to grab her hat and coat from their spot on her sleeping pallet? Now she had nothing, just the long sleeves of her dress to protect her against winter's harshness. She felt something land on her eyelashes, something else on her cheek, little cold kisses that melted against her skin. Looking up, Ivy saw that it had begun to snow.

She stopped, standing in the middle of the pavement, hugging herself against the cold. Her thoughts were slow and muddled with shock and anguish, like the way they were right after Bertha died, but she tried to consider her options. She couldn't go back to the warehouse – that much was certain. Jane was right; she was nothing but a burden, a bad influence on George, bringing her shameful past with her.

But where else was there? She thought of the ugly, squat gray buildings that they'd passed by occasionally, of how Bertha had always pulled her closer and muttered darkly, "You'll never end up in one of those workhouses, my lovely." Ivy didn't know what about them had made Bertha look so frightened, but she knew that nothing ever frightened Bertha, so the workhouse wasn't an option either.

She gazed dully around at the street. A scruffy young man was going from lamp-post to lamp-post, lighting them one by one. Everyone else was bundled up in hats and scarves, heading to their homes. For two years, Ivy had had a home of her own. It felt a long way away now, she thought, tucking her freezing hands a little deeper beneath her armpits. She and Bertha had spent their fair share of nights on the street, but with a warm body to cuddle up to, Ivy had never really known cold.

She was starting to get acquainted with it now. It was crawling deeper and deeper under her skin, sending the beginnings of a few shivers up her tired spine. She couldn't keep walking forever. With a gentle shock, Ivy realized that she wouldn't make it through the night. Not alone out here in the cold, with not even a coat or a blanket to cover her.

The knowledge would have scared her a few hours ago. Now, it just seemed to bounce off her numb consciousness. She gazed up and down the street, seeking idly for inspiration. The street was lined with shops, and one or two still had lights burning inside them. Through the window of the nearest one, Ivy watched an ugly tabby cat walk across the floor, its tail held high. It only had one eye, and its face was squashed and battle-scarred; she expected the shopkeeper to chase it off with a broom. Instead, when the cat jumped up onto the counter and rubbed against the shoulder of the plump lady who was busy talking to some customers, she absently began to stroke its scruffy fur.

Suddenly, as clearly as if she was standing beside her, Ivy heard Bertha's voice in her mind. *Kindness is a great thing to have, Ivy, but it's also a great thing to take advantage of. Kind people don't look for reasons why you're lying – they want to help you, and so you just have to give them a little story to help them help you even more.*

The words had made her giggle back then. Now, they made her feel a little sick. What would George say? She closed her eyes, picturing him at supper, pausing before their usual grace.

His line was always the same, so well-worn that Ivy heard it word for word in her head. "Now remember, everyone," he said, "the only reason we have anything to eat tonight is because a lot of people have decided to be kind to us today."

George would never take advantage of people like this.

There was a gust of wind, and an eddy of snow blew up around Ivy's legs, the wind puffing into her face. Its chill shuddered down through her skin and struck her straight in the heart with a force that she knew would quickly turn deadly.

I'm not saying stealing's a good thing, but eating is a good thing, and if we want to keep eating, we have to keep stealing. The prospect of the night out in the cold yawned before Ivy, a great abyss of fear.

Her arms and legs moved almost mechanically. It had been two years since she'd last taken anything, but it was with surprising ease that she gently bumped into one of the men walking past. As he spun around to shout at her, she lowered her eyes, closed her hand quickly over the coins she'd just slipped out of his pocket, and apologized profusely.

The next man was so engrossed in the newspaper he was reading that she was able to take his wallet without him even knowing she was there; it was the work of a few seconds to pass by again and pinch his watch as well. Within ten minutes, Ivy was in an alley, hidden among some old bins, counting out the money she had. It was enough to buy her a room in an inn for the night, but she knew that there wasn't a decent inn that would take her, not alone and not looking as scruffy as she did right now.

Cautiously, she peered out of the alley at the shopkeeper and the ugly cat. There was a sign above the door, reading *Anne Cooper Seamstress*. She remembered a trick that she and Bertha had pulled on a dressmaker when she was just a little girl and backed a little deeper into the alleyway. Working fast, Ivy grabbed her left sleeve, gritted her teeth, and ripped it off. A section of her skirt followed; then a piece of the baggy bodice of her too-big dress. She pulled a few strands loose from her hair and fluffed it up, then knelt and pressed her hands into the dirt of the alley floor, smearing it all over her face and dress. Last, gritting her teeth a little, she dug her fingernails into her cheek. The red marks were convincing enough when she checked them in a nearby frozen puddle that she knew she was ready. She quickly hid the stolen watch and wallet underneath some rubbish, hoping they'd still be there when she got back.

Taking a deep breath, she stumbled across the street, keeping a hand pressed against her cheek. Now, the glances heading her way were concerned instead of irritated. Sobbing a little – her aching feet were cause enough for crying that it didn't take much acting to get her tears flowing – she staggered up to the seamstress's shop.

The bell above the door jangled loudly as she half fell into the shop. "Please," she gasped. "Please help me."

"Good gracious, child!" The shopkeeper rushed out from behind the counter, ignoring the customers standing nearby. "What happened to you?"

Ivy softened her accent slightly, making it sound more country-like.

"I'm so sorry, ma'am," she said. "This – this city is so big, I must have taken a wrong turn. We haven't been here long, and my mama told me not to get lost, but the streets all look the same." She sniffed, allowing her tears to pour down her cheeks. "I ended up – oh, I don't know where, but the way all the men looked at me was so frightening. I just had to go to the market to buy some bread for Mama – she's a housekeeper – and – and they took all my money." She cried harder. "Look what they did to my dress."

"You poor thing!" exclaimed the shopkeeper, her eyes widening in sympathy as they traveled over her ruined dress.

"I-I'm sorry to come in here like this," Ivy said, nervously tugging at the ripped edges of her bodice. "I-I just thought I'd ask if you had a little scrap of cloth somewhere, something I could just tie around m-myself so that I could walk home safely." Her crying intensified. "I d-d-don't have a single coin left. I j-j-just know I can't walk all the way back home like this."

"Hush now, you poor lamb," said the shopkeeper, putting a maternal hand on her shoulder. "You'll be all right. Come with me. I'm sure I have an old dress somewhere that's gone out of fashion but is still quite wearable. That should get you safely home – you can't walk anywhere like this, not in this weather."

A few minutes later, wearing an old but barely worn dress in a rather flattering shade of dark blue, Ivy walked out of the shop, thanking its kindly keeper profusely for the free dress and the opportunity to wash her face and get herself cleaned up. She tucked the last of her hair back into its tie and smoothed it down as she hurried back to the alley and retrieved the wallet and watch. Then she headed straight toward the nearest inn, knowing that her new dress and a confident enough manner would be able to convince the innkeeper that she was at least fifteen years old and traveling to join the rest of her family in the city.

Once she was safely in her room, she would start working on a story filled with references and experience, ready to pitch it to housekeepers all over the wealthier part of town. If things went the way they always had with Bertha – and she was confident that they would – she would have a job before the week was out.

A sense of security started to fill her. Bertha had taught her everything she knew, and Ivy knew that she was capable of taking care of herself. Yet, despite the relief she felt, there was no pride, no joy, and no contentment. She pictured George's face if he knew what she was doing right now, and a stab of pure agony shot through her heart.

Jane was right. Ivy was nothing but a thief and a liar – and that was what she would always be.

CHAPTER 13

The dish water was deliciously warm. Ivy buried her hands into it, allowing the suds to slop around her elbows, and scrubbed a fine china plate deep inside the water, enjoying the sensation as her fingers warmed up. It had been a few days since she'd felt the biting cold that had scared her so much on that day; almost a week ago now, that she'd been thrown out of the warehouse. Still, it was a feeling she wasn't going to forget anytime soon. Every bit of warmth that she felt was a relief – from the water she was using to wash the dishes, to the radiating heat from the stove in the corner as its coals began to cool after making the sumptuous dinner that her master had just enjoyed, to the cheerful warmth from the hearth in the corner of the kitchen.

She finished washing the plate and handed it over to the girl standing next to her. Short and homely, her hair was cut level with her jawline, and she was about the same age as Ivy. It bobbed gently as she took the plate and plunged it into the rinse water.

"Thanks," she said.

Ivy gave her a curious look. "You've thanked me for every single plate," she said, smiling. "You know it's my job to wash them and pass them to you, don't you?"

The girl's smile was as pleasant as her dumpy curves. She laughed, an infectious, bubbling sound. "Sorry," she said. "I wasn't even thinking about it."

"I'm just teasing."

"And I'm Mildred." The girl grinned. "Pleased to meet you, Just Teasing."

Ivy laughed. "It's Ivy, actually," she said.

"Well, it's still nice to meet you."

Ivy stared at Mildred for a few seconds. The girl had sweet, sensible little dimples in each cheek, and a genuine warmth in her eyes that Ivy hadn't seen since the last time she waved goodbye to George. It was like seeing a spark on a dark night, and she couldn't help but run toward it. "So how long have you been working here?" Ivy asked.

Before Mildred could reply, there was a shout from somewhere in the back of the kitchen. "You! New girl!"

Ivy spun around, suds flying. The housekeeper, who was tall and rotund with a collection of ominously wobbly chins, stormed across the kitchen toward them. Her frizzy hair made her look like she'd been struck by lightning.

"What are you doing?" she demanded, pointing furiously at Ivy.

"W-washing dishes, ma'am?" Ivy stammered.

"It looks very much like you were standing around talking to me," said the housekeeper. Her eyes narrowed. "I wasn't that sure you were telling me the truth about all of your experience and recommendations, girl, but we were desperate to get extra help. Still, there are plenty of girls out there like you. I will think nothing about dismissing you."

"N-no, ma'am. Please. I'm s-sorry," Ivy began, but to her astonishment, Mildred cut in. She planted her damp hands on her abundant hips and glared up at the housekeeper.

"There's no need for that," she said. "Ivy's been up to her elbows in those dishes for hours. She's washed more in an evening than that previous girl could have washed in a week. We were just talking and working at the same time, that's all."

The housekeeper's eyes flashed. Ivy cowered, certain that Mildred was going to get a cuff alongside the ear. Instead, the housekeeper merely muttered, "Don't think that you can get away with this sort of thing just because you're my daughter, Mildred."

"I'm not trying to get away with anything, Mama," said Mildred, turning back to the dishes. "Neither of us were doing anything wrong. Come on, Ivy. Let's get the last of these done."

To Ivy's amazement, the housekeeper just gave them both a glare, then shook her head.

"I'm going to clean the parlor after the master's party," she said. "When I get back, this kitchen had better be sparkling clean – or else even you won't be able to change my mind, Mildred." She stomped out.

Ivy turned back to the dishes, and as soon as the housekeeper was gone, Mildred gave her a friendly bump with her shoulder.

"So, to answer your question," she said, "my mama is the housekeeper, while my papa is one of the grooms in the master's stables. I've been working here pretty much since I was born."

"That must be nice," said Ivy. "To stay in one place your whole life, you know."

"Well, the world does start to feel a little small after thirteen years," said Mildred, "but it's good to know where you'll be sleeping every night, anyway." She gave Ivy a curious, but empathetic, look. "I'm guessing you've been traveling around a lot."

Ivy hesitated. She couldn't tell Mildred her full story, or she'd risk giving away the fact that she'd told nothing but untruths about her past experience. "A little," she said, hesitantly.

"It's all right." Mildred's tone was gentle. "You don't have to worry about that kind of thing with me."

"Worry about what?" asked Ivy, with a light laugh.

"You know. Your past," said Mildred. "The girl who used to work here in your place, she was on the streets for a while, too."

Ivy's shoulders sagged. "Is it obvious?"

"No, not really. I guess I've just seen a lot of girls come and go from a lot of different situations," said Mildred, smiling. "So, tell me a bit more about yourself, new girl."

"There's not much to tell," said Ivy. "My mama and papa were never a part of my life, but instead, my auntie raised me." Her voice thickened a little at the mention of Bertha. "She was wonderful. I loved her very much – and she loved me even more."

"That sounds nice," said Mildred. "Where did you stay?"

"Oh... sort of everywhere," said Ivy. She felt a twist of guilt in her stomach and quickly went on, hoping that Mildred wouldn't ask about what Bertha had done for work. "But my auntie passed on about two years ago. Then I lived with some children in an old abandoned warehouse." She gave a tiny sigh.

"That sounds like it was hard," said Mildred sympathetically.

"It was hard work, sometimes, but it was actually good," said Ivy. "I was very good friends with the leader of the group. His name was... *is*... George. George Taylor. He was the wisest, kindest person I ever knew. There was nothing I couldn't tell him and nothing that we couldn't talk about. And we spent so much time together..." Ivy's voice trailed off.

"So, what happened to him?" asked Mildred gently.

"Nothing. Well... there was a falling out." Ivy swallowed, shaking her head. "I realized that I just... wasn't good for him or for the group. So I left."

"I'm sorry to hear that," said Mildred. "It sounds like you cared for him."

"I did. I do," said Ivy. "But it's for the best. I'm never, ever going to go back there – not even to walk past." She forced a smile. "I'm here now, at any rate."

Mildred took her damp hands out of the water and put one on Ivy's arm. Her grin was warm, genuine, and gentle. "Yes, you are," she said. "And I'm going to take care of you, all right?"

Ivy returned her smile. "That's all right with me," she said.

CHAPTER 14

Ivy was going to regret what she was doing.

It was her second Sunday off – although it was technically only a half-Sunday, being just three hours in the afternoon. Still, those three hours could get very long if one didn't know what to do with oneself. Or if one knew exactly what one wanted to do, but that doing it would be as wrong as it was painful.

She'd known that it was a mistake to go wandering in the streets. Nothing good could come of it; she might see one of the gang of children, even though George generally kept them all at home in the warehouse on a Sunday, sharing scraps of food and resting. She'd known that eventually, inevitably, her feet would start to carry her down toward the warehouse district. The walk was familiar; she'd spent many hours begging or singing on the streets near the wealthy area where she now worked. Before she knew it, she was walking in between the looming hulks of the abandoned warehouses, their empty windows staring down at her like the eye sockets in skulls.

The broken window was still as it had been three years ago when she and Bertha had first started hiding out in the warehouse. Quick and quiet, careful not to tear her relatively new dress, Ivy slipped inside and soundlessly moved across the tops of the boxes. Now and then, she paused to listen to the voices down below: Jane's snapping, Joan piping, Peter and Timmy laughing as they wrestled one another.

Then she heard him. George. His pure voice rising above the rest, glowing as golden as his hair. "Come on, Freddy," he was saying gently. "It's all right. It's not too hot, see? I've blown on it – you can take it."

Lying on her belly, Ivy crawled across to the edge of the boxes and peered down into the circle of light where the children stayed – where she had stayed, only a few weeks ago. An unfamiliar little boy was sitting on the edge of his sleeping pallet, and George knelt in front of him, holding a small bowl of hot soup and a spoon.

"Go on," George said, holding out the spoon. "It's for you."

Slowly, the little boy took a bite. Ivy saw his eyes widen. Then he grabbed the bowl and started eating for himself in huge, ravenous gulps. George smiled, ruffling the little boy's hair. "That's it," he said. "Well done."

Getting up, George stretched his legs slowly, as if he'd been kneeling in front of his new little charge for a long time. He stretched the kinks out of his back and neck before walking over to where Jane was sitting on her own sleeping pallet some way away. The other children were running and shouting, playing a rowdy game of tag on the other side of the warehouse.

"He's eating, at least," George said, sitting down on another pallet nearby. "I think he might be sick, though. His little body felt so terribly hot when I picked him up out of the gutter."

"He'd better not make the rest of us sick," said Jane. "What will we do if half of them come down with something?"

"We'll nurse them back to health, just like we did when everyone caught colds in that sudden rainstorm a few months ago," said George. He sighed, his shoulders suddenly slumping. "It would be a lot easier if Ivy was around to help, though."

Jane sat up, bristling. "Why would you even mention her?" she snapped. "She left. Ivy abandoned us, George. I can't believe you still even think about her."

"I think about her all the time." George sounded genuinely shocked. "She was one of us, Jane. I can't believe she just

disappeared the way she did." He sighed. "I still miss her –
and I'm still worried for her. We searched all of these streets
for her, but there was just no sign. How could she vanish into
thin air like that?" He groaned, pushing his hands into his
hair. "Would someone have taken her? Is she hurt and scared
or alone somewhere? I miss her so much, Jane. And I wish I
knew that she was all right."

George's words made Ivy's heart hammer. She lurched to her
knees, trying to find her feet. He did miss her. He did want
her – Jane had been wrong about everything. She was about to
run down to the bottom of the circle, to scream George's
name, to throw herself into his arms when Jane's voice
cracked like a snapping whip.

"She was a thief and a liar!" Jane got to her feet, her hands
balling into fists. "Didn't I tell you many times already that
she took almost all of our cheese from the stockpile? I told
you that she was untrustworthy from the beginning – and she
proved it!"

Ivy froze. Her heart felt like it had been turned to ice, then
shattered brutally with a vengeful hammer. She hadn't taken
anything from the stockpile, but she looked down at her new
dark blue dress, and agony blossomed in her as she realized
that Jane was right. She was a thief. She had stolen and lied
her way into the position she had now. How could she ever
explain that to George?

How could she ever explain that to anyone?

Ivy didn't wait to hear George's response. She heard the last notes of his voice follow her, like light bouncing above the piles of junk, as she fled.

"Ivy? What's the matter?"

Ivy held her breath. She'd hoped that she'd kept her sniffles quiet enough that Mildred wouldn't hear. Squeezing her eyes tight shut, she forced herself to take a couple of deep, shuddering breaths. Maybe Mildred would think that she was asleep and leave her alone. Or maybe she would come and see, come and ask what it was that was breaking Ivy's heart. Ivy wasn't sure which one she was hoping for.

"Ivy?" Mildred said again.

Ivy squeezed her eyes a little tighter and felt a tear run, hot and damp, down her cheek. She tried to take another deep breath, but this time, it caught, and her sob echoed through the little room that she shared with her new friend.

"Oh, Ivy, what is it?" Mildred's blanket rustled as she pushed it back and hurried across the tiny room to Ivy's bed. Its wooden frame squeaked as Mildred knelt down beside it, and Ivy felt her hand feeling around in the dark until it rested on Ivy's shoulder.

"Why are you crying?" she whispered.

Ivy tried to get the words out. "I-I... George..." But she hardly knew what to say. What had changed? Nothing – she had just been reminded of how bad a person she was. Of how little she deserved.

"Shhh." Mildred climbed up, sitting on the bed with Ivy, and started gently stroking her hair. "Hush now. It's all right. Whatever happened with George, I'm here now. And I'm going to be your friend, all right? I'm going to be your friend always."

Ivy began to cry, and suddenly, she couldn't stop. It felt as though the well of tears inside her had no bottom. They flowed all over her face, her hands, her pillow, her blanket, and Mildred didn't move, slowly and rhythmically stroking Ivy's hair.

"It's all right," she kept saying. "I'm here. I'm right here."

She sounded like Bertha. She sounded like home. And eventually, it was the sound of her voice that led Ivy into a deep and dreamless sleep.

IVY HAD DISCOVERED A NEW HIDING PLACE. IN THE MIDDLE of one of the piles of old boxes and other nameless junk, Ivy was all but invisible to the children that were resting and playing in the circle that George had hollowed out for them. If she pressed her face against a crack in one of the boxes, though, she could watch them, and their voices penetrated the heap of rubbish that sheltered her little hiding place.

It had become a habit, even though every week she promised herself that she'd never go back to the warehouse. Every Sunday, after washing the lunch dishes from her master's family, she would take her own lunch – usually a chunk of bread – and wander through the streets until she reached the place that had once been her home. Then she would hide and watch. She knew now that she could never let George see her again, but she also knew that she couldn't go without hearing his voice now and then and knowing that he was still George and that he was all right.

He certainly looked all right now. He was standing in front of a group of the children, listening as their sweet little voices rose high into the air, the notes fumbling at times, but their harmony poignant to hear. George watched approvingly, nodding as they sang.

"Three little boats went sailing out into the west, out into the sea when the stars came out." Their small voices formed the words carefully, some of them a little hesitant as they reached for the higher notes. "Each little boat thought he was the best, and the town watched them float and bob, float and bob."

As the children sang, Ivy kept her eyes trained on George. The intensity of his gaze on the children made her heart skip a beat, and his smile broadened as they made their way through the song.

"Three little boats all smashed into the rock," they went on. "But the fishies came, the fishies came..."

The song stuttered. Joan, who had been bravely leading it, suddenly stopped. In a mumble of voices, the children ground to a halt. "I'm sorry, George." Joan's eyes were wide. "I – I forgot the next word."

"It's all right!" George grinned. "You're doing fine. I'll help you." He raised his own voice, rising like organ pipes through the warehouse, turning its gloom into the splendor of a cathedral. "And the fishes recused the boats, the boats, the boats," he sang, "and saved the sailors one and all."

The children all joined him again as they reached the last refrain. "And now it's time to bring the sails, bring the sails, bring the sails..."

Ivy was listening, entranced by the sound of George's voice, her half-forgotten bread clutched in her hand, when suddenly the hands seized her. Strong arms wound around her throat, hands clapping over her mouth and muffling her scream.

Instinctively, she kicked out, but it was no good – she was being dragged deeper into the rubbish, helpless, her knees and elbows banging on the floor as she fought to get free. Her nostrils were filled with the smell of some foul, unwashed body, and the strength with which she was being dragged across the floor was utterly terrifying.

As suddenly as she'd been grabbed, Ivy was let go. She fell to the ground, her bread tumbling out of her fingers, and tried to run, but tripped over an outstretched leg and slammed down onto her face.

"Get her!" barked a rough voice. Ivy rolled onto her back and saw them: three boys, all older than George, their faces filthy, their clothes reeking of the sewage. The look in their eyes terrified her. She tried to bolt, but they were quicker, grabbing her arms, her skin sliding through their sweaty hands. Fingers clutched at her dress, her hair, a hand closing over her mouth again, and Ivy knew nothing but utter terror. She thrashed, their strength effortlessly restraining her. There was a filthy finger against her mouth, and she had no choice. She opened her mouth, braced herself for the disgusting reality of it all, and bit down as hard as she could. Her teeth met flesh, and one of her attackers yowled, letting her go.

"Help!" Ivy screamed. "HELP!"

She heard George's voice shouting, and it sent a jolt of terror through her. What had she done? It was enough to help her twist free, and her startled attackers' hands fell away from her. She was free. Ignoring the pain of her bruised limbs, Ivy bolted, scrambling through the rubbish, her dress ripping on old nails and bits of wire, not caring. She had to get away.

She had to run before George saw her.

"STOP!" George was shouting. He'd spotted the boys. "What are you doing here? GET THEM! STOP THEM!"

The other children were shouting, but Ivy didn't have time to listen. She'd reached the broken window. As quick as she could, she tumbled through it, just like she had the day that she'd stolen from George's stockpile. Only this time, she didn't hide or hesitate. She just ran, as fast as her legs could carry her.

Ivy's knees still stung from the beating those ruffians had given her almost two weeks before, but she couldn't bring herself to care as she knelt on the kitchen floor, scrubbing at the stains of a week's cooking. She could see Mildred shooting her worried glances from the other side of the kitchen, where she was following up Ivy's scrubbing with her mop, but they couldn't talk now – not with the cook and housekeeper finishing up the stew.

Ivy tried to ignore Mildred's looks. She didn't think she had the strength to tell Mildred why she was so exhausted, so upset today – or why she'd cried herself to sleep again the night before. The bruises that the ruffians who'd stolen her bread the week before had given her had already almost healed. But what she felt in her heart was a gaping wound, a pit of agony that she had to keep herself away from in case she fell in and couldn't get out.

She'd almost finished her scrubbing when the cook and housekeeper left, carrying breakfast out to the family. Almost at once, Mildred planted her mop back in the bucket and hurried over to Ivy, kneeling in front of her.

"All right, Ivy," she said. "You've got to tell me. What's going on? What happened to you at that warehouse yesterday?" She reached out and touched Ivy's shoulder. "Was it those men who stole your bread last time? Did they... did they hurt you somehow?"

"No." Ivy shook her head, tears threatening to overwhelm her. "They weren't there."

"They weren't there?" Mildred frowned. "So why are you so upset?"

"You don't understand." Ivy dropped her scrubbing brush back in the bucket and sat back, burying her face in her hands. "George and the others. The whole gang. They weren't there."

The words brought the previous afternoon back to her with a piercing pain. She'd been nervous as she hurried toward the warehouse, keeping an eye out for the thieves, but there had been no sign of them. She guessed George and the others must have driven them out. At least, so she'd hoped – until she reached the warehouse and found the circle of light to be completely empty. No sleeping pallets, no stockpile, and definitely no children. It was swept as clean as if they had never existed. As if Ivy had imagined George, and he'd suddenly disappeared out of her dreams.

"Gone?" Mildred put an arm around Ivy's shoulders. "Maybe they'd just gone out somewhere. To beg or something, like you told me they did."

"No, Mildred." Ivy shook her head, forcing the words out in between her tears. "They'd taken everything. They're not coming back." She gulped. "When I was still with them, George used to talk about what we'd do if a violent gang moved into the area – he had a whole plan for getting the little children out of there. Everyone knew who would carry what and who would look after the little ones. He was so ready..." She swallowed, tears pouring down her cheeks. "That must have been what happened. Those men who beat me up must have scared them off."

"Didn't he say where you'd go?" Mildred asked gently.

"No. He hadn't decided yet. He was still... still looking for places when Jane... when I left." Ivy had to sob for a few more moments before she could squeeze the terrible truth past the lump in her throat. "George is gone, Mildred. He's gone, and I will never, ever see him again."

PART IV

CHAPTER 15

Ivy worked the polish over the silver spoon, her cloth sliding to and fro easily over its tarnished surface. Trying to pay attention to her work, she scrubbed away, but it was difficult now that she was laughing so hard. "Mildred, stop," she pleaded. "I'm supposed to get all of this silver polished, and you're not making it any easier."

"I'm sorry," said Mildred, wiping away tears of laughter. "It was just so funny – you should have seen that new stable boy's face. It was like he'd never even seen a horse before. When that gelding stood on my papa's foot as he was lecturing the boy about how to keep from getting trodden on, it was just hilarious."

"I can only imagine," said Ivy, laughing. "But you'd better help me with this silver if you want to get everything done, or we'll be in trouble with your mother."

"Then you've got to help me with the pots," countered Mildred, her eyes dancing. "One hand washes the other, and all that."

Ivy laughed, shaking her head. Somehow, Mildred could brighten up even the dullest of tasks, like getting the kitchen ready for one of the master's countless dinner parties. Even the housekeeper, who was sitting at the kitchen table and writing a list of the things they needed, couldn't help but chuckle now and then as the two girls bantered. She'd come to accept their friendship, if a little begrudgingly.

Ivy put the polished spoon aside and reached for a dirty one. She could hear Mildred pause in scouring the pots behind her.

"You know," Mildred said, "I think this Sunday afternoon we should go out and buy a new dress."

"You do?" said Ivy.

"Yes, I do. Well, you know – not quite new, but new to us. We're the same size, so we can share it. Then we each have half a new dress."

"But nothing will be open on a Sunday," Ivy pointed out.

"But we have a friend with a shop..."

"Do you?" Ivy smiled. "But I don't think you'd get very far with just half a dress, Mildred. What would people think?"

"Oh, you know what I mean!" Mildred grinned.

There was a knock at the door to the servant's quarters. Mildred immediately fell silent, turning around, a mixture of hope and expectation on her face. "I'll go and see," said the housekeeper, getting up. "Can't have one of you two little slips heading out by yourselves."

There was obvious disappointment on Mildred's face. As soon as the housekeeper was out of the kitchen, Ivy gave Mildred a wink. "It's a bit late for your beloved paper-boy, don't you think?" she said.

Mildred colored immediately. "I – I don't know what you're talking about," she said.

Ivy laughed. "That's quite surprising, considering what a pretty color you've just gone."

"Bobby is only a friend," said Mildred defensively.

"Yes, and you jump every time there's a knock at the door because you're so excited to see someone who is only a friend," teased Ivy.

"Oh, all right." Mildred raised her hands to her cheeks, trying to cover up her blush, and gave a girlish giggle. "Maybe I do have a little bit of an eye on him. But oh, Ivy, haven't you seen him? He has such wonderfully green eyes. I've never seen eyes so green. It looks like someone put two emeralds into his head."

"Yes, and you just gaze into them romantically as you slowly take the paper from him," said Ivy, clutching her hands underneath her chin. "The highlight of your day."

"Ivy!" Mildred laughed, throwing the pot-scourer at her. Ivy dodged. "It's true!" she protested.

Mildred's expression softened. She leaned on the sink, cocking her head to one side. "You know, in all the four years that we've been friends, I've never heard you talk about a boy even once," she said. "And you're almost seventeen already."

Ivy looked away. "There's only ever been one boy for me, Mildred," she said softly. "And I'll never see him again."

"Surely you don't want to be an old maid, though," said Mildred.

"It doesn't matter to me." Ivy shook her head. "If it's not him, then it doesn't matter. I'd rather be alone than with anyone else."

Mildred sighed. "George must have been very special," she said, "for you to love him this much."

Ivy closed her eyes. It had been so many years since she'd last seen George. She'd grown from a little girl into a young woman; he would be a man by now, fully grown. Did he have a beard? Were his shoulders even broader, his voice even deeper than when she'd last seen him? Had he found his way out of the life he'd been trying to keep together for the other children? The fact that she'd never know hurt her heart every single day.

"Trust me," she said softly. "He was the most special person I ever knew." She opened her eyes and gazed fondly at her friend. "Maybe except for you, of course."

Mildred laughed. "Stop flattering me and get back to those spoons," she said, her voice light.

Ivy bent to pick up the scourer that Mildred had thrown at her. She'd just straightened up when the housekeeper came in again, a strange expression on her face. "It's for you," she said.

Ivy stared at her blankly. "Excuse me, ma'am?"

"The person at the door." The housekeeper folded her arms. "A very scruffy-looking little person, too, I might add. She says she's looking for you – Ivy Harris."

Ivy and Mildred exchanged glances. "Who could it be?" asked Mildred.

"I have no idea," said Ivy. "I don't know anyone outside of this house."

"Well, you'd best go and speak to them and get them to go away," said the housekeeper, "because that's what I told her, only she wouldn't go away. She insisted on seeing you."

"You'd better go and check," said Mildred.

Confused, Ivy wiped her hands on a dishcloth and walked

toward the servant's door. When she opened it, for a moment, her entire world stood still.

Jane.

The older girl had grown even taller now, but her frame had remained as scrawny as ever despite the curves that had been added to her figure. She wore a shawl with a hood that she had pulled close over her face, and her eyes darted this way and that, dark and quick. When she saw Ivy, her mouth twisted with distaste.

Her presence brought all of the bad memories flooding back. Ivy stepped back, ready to slam the door and tell everyone that she had no idea who it was, but Jane shot forward, grabbing the doorknob. Then she uttered the single word that Ivy was least expecting. "Please."

Ivy stopped, staring at her. "What do you want, Jane?" she asked flatly. "How did you even know where to find me?"

"Because one time I followed you. You're not the only one who sneaks around. Trust me, I wouldn't have come here if I had any other choice," said Jane.

Ivy's eyes narrowed. "What do you mean?"

"We need you. I..." Jane gritted her teeth, frowning. "I need you."

"*You* need *me?*" Ivy folded her arms. "You said that I was a thief and a liar, nothing but a burden, but you were always telling George how we should have been stealing. So make up your mind. What is it now?"

Jane looked away, staring down into the street. The pause between them stretched like a violin string, tight and uncomfortable, for a long moment. When Jane looked back up, Ivy was startled to see that her eyes were filled with tears.

"It's George," she cried.

"What?" Ivy felt as though her blood had stopped pounding inside her body. She took a step nearer, suddenly scared by the tears in Jane's eyes. "What is it? What about him?"

Jane swallowed. It took her a while to summon up the words, dredging them from some dark and frightened corner of her soul.

"He's dying," she said. "You'd better come."

Ivy's heart hammered. Jane's words were like a bucket of ice water over the top of her head, but with the cold clarity of someone who'd just been woken from a four-year-long dream, Ivy knew exactly what she had to do.

"We'll be found out if I come now," she said, surprised by the calm in her own voice. "Do you think he can hang on until nightfall?"

Jane nodded. "But not much longer. I'll meet you here around nine o' clock." She took a deep breath, her eyes still fixed on Ivy's with a mixture of hope and repugnance. "Don't be late."

CHAPTER 16

Ivy sat on the edge of her sleeping pallet, staring through the crack in her room's door at the clock on the kitchen wall. It read five to nine at last; it had felt as though the afternoon would drag by for decades. She felt as though she might explode from the weight of the questions bouncing around inside her. What had happened to George? Where was he?

And why, of all people, had Jane come to her?

She glanced across at Mildred. Their single, stubby candle was balanced on the floor beside Mildred's bed, and she was engrossed in reading a piece of the newspaper. Between Ivy and her mother, they'd succeeded in teaching her something. Forcing herself to be casual, Ivy rose to her feet, taking her coat from the foot of her bed.

"I need some air," she said. "I'll be right back."

Mildred sat up. "I'll come too," she said.

"No," said Ivy, rather too sharply. Hurrying to fix her mistake, she quickly added, "It's all right. It's – um – it's a bit chilly out. I – I know you've got a bit of a cold in your nose."

Mildred gave her a sharp look. "My nose is fine. It has been for days," she said. "And it's the middle of summer." She folded her arms. "When are you going to tell me who was at the door?"

"I told you," said Ivy. "It was no one. When I opened the door, there was nobody there. It must have been some prankster."

"You can't lie to me, Ivy." Mildred raised her chin, and Ivy could see that she was hurt. "It doesn't work on me. I know you're not telling me the truth, and I don't understand why."

Ivy paused, studying her friend. "It's... it's to do with my past," she said at last. "I don't want to drag you into it, because it's dangerous and..." She sighed, getting up and pulling on her coat. "You deserve better."

"You're going to tell me what I deserve?" Mildred snorted, reaching for her own coat. "Wherever you're going, I'm coming with you."

"No, you're not," said Ivy. "It's going to be dangerous."

"All the more reason why you shouldn't go alone," said Mildred.

Ivy looked up at the clock. It was one minute to nine, and she was terrified that Jane would leave if she was even a second late. With a sinking feeling, she realized that it was no good – her friend was too stubborn.

"Oh, all right," she said. "But come quickly and quietly – and do exactly what I say. You taught me all about working in the house, but I'm the one who knows the streets."

The two girls slipped out, padding through the kitchen toward the servant's entrance. Jane was waiting for them there, her tall figure almost invisible beneath a gnarled old oak tree standing just outside.

"There you are," she said, as Ivy and Mildred came outside. Her eyes flashed with suspicion. "And who's this?"

"This is Mildred," said Ivy. "My friend. She's come to help."

Jane snorted. "She's going to be no good. Get back into your cozy little house, girl."

"I'm tougher than I look," said Mildred defiantly. "Now, where are we going?"

Jane gave Mildred a long stare before apparently deciding that arguing with her would be no use. "All right," she said, shrugging. "It's nothing to me if you get yourself into trouble. Come on. Follow me."

Jane headed onto the street, walking fast, her shoes silent on the pavement. Behind her, Ivy almost had to run to keep up, and Mildred was quickly out of breath. "Where are we going?" she hissed to Ivy.

"I don't know," said Ivy.

"Then why are we going there?" asked Mildred.

"Because of George." Ivy swallowed. "Jane says that he's sick. Very, very sick. I have to help him."

"George?" Mildred's eyes widened. She puffed, trotting to keep up. "Your old beau, George?"

Jane looked sharply over her shoulder, and Ivy felt her gaze straight into her soul. "He... he wasn't my beau," she said. "But yes. That George."

Breathless from the fast pace, Mildred fell silent for the rest of the walk. They went down into the same district as the old warehouse had been, even passing by the same building; Ivy tried not to look up at it, but she couldn't help thinking of Bertha's bones lying up there on the second floor so long ago. She shook off the spooky thought, keeping her eyes fixed on Jane.

"How much further?" she called.

"Almost there," said Jane. "When a group of ruffians moved into our area, we had to go, but George found us a spot in a warehouse not far from the old one."

True to Jane's word, a few minutes of brisk walking later, she turned right and ducked through a hole in the door of another abandoned warehouse. Mildred gave a little yelp of alarm, but Ivy didn't have time to worry about her; she knew that George was just ahead of them, and that he was suffering somehow.

She crawled quickly through the hole on her hands and knees, tugging at her skirt to prevent it from getting caught on the splintered planks that surrounded the edges of the hole. Straightening up, she wiped her hands on her skirt, smearing it with a sticky grime from the warehouse floor.

The inside of the warehouse was almost perfectly dark. Instead of the cheerful fire that had flickered in the old warehouse, there was just a lantern here, casting a watery glow around a set of pale faces that stared up at Ivy from a tight cluster of sleeping pallets. Ivy sniffed. The warehouse had a stench of old tallow; she guessed it must have been used for making candles. Everyone was sooty and grubby, and four years older than the last time she'd seen them, but she could recognize some of the older ones. Joan, now growing up into a young woman; little Gordon, now almost a man, his jaw dusted with stubble. And, lying nearest the lantern, his eyes closed, George.

"George!" Ivy gasped.

Her legs darted forward of their own accord. She rushed to

his side, falling to her knees, grasping for his hand. It flopped limply in hers, his skin hot and dry as she clutched his fingers in her own. He didn't respond. His hair was darkened with sweat, so that it looked more like flax than gold now; it was longer than ever, tumbling on the folded coat that he was using for a pillow. His beard, too, had grown; it was full of thick, golden curls now. But his face was the same: sweet, kind, the expression still gentle despite the flush of illness in his cheeks.

"Oh, he looks so sick," said Mildred, her fear vanishing in the face of sympathy. She knelt down beside Ivy, touching George's brow. Ivy didn't have to feel it to know that it was burning. His hand in hers was like holding smoldering coal. She stroked some of his hair back out of his face, her heart squeezing as she saw the dark circles under his eyes.

"What happened to him?" she asked, looking up at Jane.

Jane's eyes darted away, her face coloring again with something that might have been shame. "I was on a street corner, begging," she said, "when a group of young men came up to me. They grabbed me and dragged me into an alley and..." She took a sharp breath. "Bad things would have happened, but George heard me. He came running and fought them off, but one of them had a piece of broken glass that he used as a knife." She gestured at George's left leg. "He cut him," she said simply.

Ivy turned, pulling away the blanket that George had been covered with. She smelt the leg before she even saw it; a purulent stench that made her stomach turn. The sight was not much better. Although it was wrapped with some dirty rags, the wound had oozed yellowing pus straight through its covering.

"Oh," said Mildred, softly. Ivy heard both fear and disgust in her friend's voice. She felt the same, but she pushed it aside. "It's oozing," she said. "That's where the fever's coming from." She looked up at Jane. "He's very sick."

"I know," snapped Jane. "Why do you think I told you he was dying?"

Ivy moved back to George's shoulders. She took his hand in hers and laid her hand on his cheek. It was so hot that she almost flinched. She wished he would open his eyes again, wished that she could gaze into their gentle depths and ask him if he'd missed her as much as she'd been missing him for all these years. Sometimes she'd wondered if she had made George more perfect and lovely in her memories than he really was, but now she knew that the opposite was true: all her fond memories could not hold how wonderful he was.

"What have you been doing, all this time?" she murmured, more to him than anyone else.

Jane answered. "The same as always," she said, her voice tinged with exasperation. She knelt, putting a hand on George's shoulder. "Looking after the children. Some of the others left – Penny and Peter. They got jobs. They have better lives now. But not George."

Ivy glanced over at her. "And not you."

Jane shrugged.

It was Mildred who spoke next. "You know," she said, slowly, "I've seen this before." She touched Ivy's arm. "Do you remember, Ivy? When the young master had the hunting accident and cut his arm, and it got pus-filled, too. He was sick just like this when his friends brought him back from the hunting lodge."

Ivy nodded. "I remember. The mistress was so angry that they'd waited so long before bringing him home."

"But he got better, remember?" said Mildred. "They put poultices on the wound and gave him medicine and fed him when they could."

"He did get well." Ivy looked up at Mildred. "What are you saying?"

"I'm saying we could save him," said Mildred, her eyes wide. "We could bring him back to the house and hide him in the servants' quarters – there's that empty room near ours where no one ever goes. It's cleaner there and easier to get food and water to him. I could go tomorrow – it's Sunday – and take the money we were going to use for a new dress and ask the apothecary what we could give him."

"You'd do that for him?" Ivy whispered.

Mildred smiled, putting her hand on Ivy's shoulder. "I'd do that for you," she said. "You're my best friend."

"You'll be lucky to just be dismissed if you're caught," said Jane.

"Well, we'll have to make sure we don't get caught," said Mildred simply.

"We'd be breaking all the rules," said Ivy. "All your mother's rules."

Mildred shrugged. "What choice do we have?" she said. "Is it better to let him die here?"

Ivy gazed down at George, and her whole heart felt like it might jump inside him if it would give him the chance to survive.

"No," she whispered. "It isn't."

"Then that's settled." Mildred got up. "Come on. We'll have to make a sort of a sledge to pull him along with, or we'll never get him back there."

Ivy looked across at Jane. "We'll need to work together," she said, holding George's hand a little tighter.

Jane's eyes traveled from Ivy's face to her fingers, interlocked with George's. Ivy saw her shoulders slump in what could have been defeat.

"I suppose we will," she said, softly. "Whatever it takes to save him."

At last, they could agree on something. Ivy nodded. "Whatever it takes," she said.

CHAPTER 17

George's skin was so hot that Ivy half expected him to start smoldering where he lay. She felt the cloth that she'd laid on his forehead only a few minutes ago. It was already almost dry, and just as warm as he was. Swallowing her fear, she grabbed it and swilled it around in the bucket of lukewarm water beside the bed before wringing it out and laying it back on his brow.

"Was it warm already?" asked Mildred. Ivy looked at her where she sat on the opposite side of the bed, gently patting George's arms and legs with another damp cloth. She looked as tired and pale as her voice sounded.

"Burning up," said Ivy, hearing some of her fear leaking into her voice. "He's just getting hotter and hotter, Mildred. I don't know if..."

She couldn't say the terrible possibility out loud. Mildred

reached across and grabbed Ivy's arm. "Don't say it," she said. "It isn't over until it goes one way or the other. As long as he's breathing, we're going to look after him – you know that. We carried him all the way from that warehouse to here, risked everything smuggling him inside, kept him quiet when he had fever dreams, even found a way to nurse him without letting anyone get suspicious about our work. We spent all our money on medicine. We've been looking after him for three days." Mildred's eyes were steady. "We're not going to give up now, and neither is he."

Ivy reached for George's hand. It burned in her palm, weak and motionless. "I don't know," she whispered. "I don't know if it isn't too late."

"It's not too late until he's dead," said Mildred, bluntly. "Come on, Ivy. We've just got to keep fighting with him."

Ivy nodded, taking another cloth from the bucket and wiping George's neck and bare chest with it. She paused with her hand over his heart, feeling it beat against her skin. It was almost fluttering now, the strong thump that she remembered from the times he'd hugged her reduced to a broken stutter, like a bird beating its wings against the bars of its cage. His breathing, too, seemed to be barely happening, his chest moving a fraction of an inch up and down. Every exhalation sent a puff of hot air against Ivy's arm. She found herself staring at his chest, willing each breath out of him.

"My auntie died in my arms," she whispered.

Mildred look up, sorrow and sympathy mingling in her expression. "I'm sorry, Ivy," she said softly.

"She died in her sleep. I was holding her," said Ivy, tears flooding into her eyes and throat. "She was the sunshine in my life, and when she died, it felt like there was no light at all left in the world. None. It felt like there was no reason to be alive anymore." She swallowed, stroking George's arm. "Then George found me crying beside my auntie's body, and he led me away into a new world. He was my only hope. He is..." She had to pause; her throat choked by a noose of tears. "He is my only hope," she said at last.

"And we're going to save him," said Mildred. "Just you watch. He's going to be all right."

"I don't know." Tears gushed down Ivy's cheeks. She held George's hand in both of her own, interlacing her fingers with his, and leaned her head desperately against his chest. "I just don't know, Mildred."

She allowed the tears to flow through her, not sobbing, just letting her grief and terror drip onto the thin mattress and seep into the front of her dress as she clung to George's empty hand with everything she had. If desperation could have given him life, he would have jumped up from the bed and danced with energy. Instead he just lay there, each breath a small miracle, and Ivy leaned her head against him, listening to the rapid thump of his heart...

IVY MUST HAVE SLEPT, BECAUSE THE NEXT THING SHE KNEW, she was waking. Mildred was clutching her shoulder, shaking her gently. "Ivy. Ivy, wake up."

Ivy sat up, gasping, her hands tightening convulsively over George's. Her eyes flew to his face, and for a moment, her heart stuttered. The skin that had been so flushed was pale now. The hand in hers that had burned with fever was now cold. She remembered how Bertha's hand had felt after she'd died. Ice cold, and growing slowly stiffer—

"George," Ivy gasped, tears pouring down her cheeks. "Oh, George!"

"Shhh. Ivy. Ivy!" Mildred looked into her eyes. "It's all right. Look. Feel him." She pressed the back of her hand to George's forehead. "It's gone, Ivy. It's gone."

That was when Ivy saw the sweat beading on George's upper lip. Hardly daring to hope, she pressed her fingertips into his wrist. His pulse thudded against her fingers, stronger, steady, fearless.

The fever had broken.

IVY KEPT THE BREAD AND CHEESE, WRAPPED IN A NAPKIN, carefully hidden in her coat as she hurried down the narrow passageway into the servants' quarters. She checked behind her twice, making sure that she wasn't being followed, before reaching the small room at the very end of the passage. Checking over her shoulder one more time, Ivy raised her hand and gave a rhythmic little knock before gently opening the door.

George was awake. He sat up in his bed, his healing leg propped up on a pillow. His face lit up when he saw Ivy.

"Hello," he said, keeping his voice quiet. "Is it lunch time already?"

"A little early," said Ivy, unable to keep the smile off her face. She grabbed the piece of plank that they were using as a tray from behind the door and placed it on George's knees. "Sorry about that. You might have a long wait between lunch and dinner – the housekeeper has been keeping us busy today, so I sneaked away the first chance I got, in case I didn't get to come later."

George watched, frowning, as Ivy opened the napkin onto the makeshift tray. "I still think I should go back to the warehouse," he said. "Every time you girls come down this passage, you're putting yourselves at risk for me."

"You know that's out of the question," said Ivy. She placed her hand on George's arm, looking into his eyes. His face was still pale and bony. "You're still too weak. It's only been a few days since your fever broke."

George's gentle, dark eyes were so deep that Ivy felt she might fall into them, might go tumbling into their depths and lose herself in the vastness of his compassion.

"You saved my life," he murmured. "Why did you disappear, all those years ago, only to come back into my life just when I needed you the most?"

Ivy looked away. "I wasn't good for the group," she said quietly. "I was nothing but a little thief." She looked shamefully at the food she'd smuggled out of the kitchens for him. "Maybe I still am."

"I don't understand," said George.

"Don't worry." Ivy forced a smile. She sat down, perched on the edge of the bed, and her hand found his. Their fingers interlocked. "I'm here now, for as long as you need me," she said.

George's eyes didn't leave hers. "I've needed you ever since you left," he said. "I missed you so much, Ivy. I was looking everywhere for you."

"George—"

"Shhh. It's all right." George reached out, pressing his finger to her lips. Spellbound, Ivy just blinked at him, suddenly unable to move. "You don't need to explain anything to me. I'm just so glad that you're back. And I'm grateful for everything you and Mildred have been doing for me." He let his hand fall back onto the bed and glanced ruefully at his injured leg. "You saved me."

"I'm just returning a favor," said Ivy softly. "You rescued me when Aunt Bertha died, too."

"I couldn't have left you there," said George.

Ivy couldn't help it. She reached out and touched his cheek, her fingers brushing against the thick curls of his beard. His eyes were so deep, and she felt like she could spend her whole day gazing into them. "Nor could I have left you," she whispered.

George turned his head slightly, leaning into her touch, but his eyes didn't leave hers. She wanted to pull him closer, gazing at the lips that were half-hidden by a golden thatch of beard, wondering how they would feel on hers...

There was a shout from the kitchen, and Ivy pulled back. George cleared his throat, leaning back onto his pillows. "I-I had better go," said Ivy awkwardly, getting up. "I think they're looking for me."

"Go," said George. "I'll see you later. Thank you for the lunch... and for everything."

Ivy paused in the doorway, gazing at him. She wanted to drink him in, to never let him out of her sight again, not after missing him for four aching years. "Thank *you*, George," she whispered, and hurried away.

IT HAD BEEN A LONG DAY. IVY'S ARMS WERE TIRED FROM scrubbing, her hands chapped and dry, and she still had a long way to go before she could rest. She tried to ignore her tired muscles as she moved quietly around the parlor, picking up dirty cups and saucers holding nothing but cake crumbs, then placing them neatly on her tray. Her mind wandered to George, as it had been doing all day. Was he still all right, secreted away in the little room?

There were two men sitting in front of the hearth. One, her master, gave his glass of wine an appreciative sniff before sipping at it. The other was gazing into the fire, turning his glass this way and that in his hand, his eyes faraway. Ivy took his plate from beside his elbow as quietly as she could, not wanting to interrupt his reverie. She noticed some spilled chocolate on the carpet near the settee and knelt by it, quickly scrubbing at it with a cloth.

"How are the children?" the thoughtful man asked.

The master took another sip of wine. "They're well, thank you. James has just graduated from medical school – we're happy to have another doctor in the family. Lucretia's studies are not going as well as we'd hoped, but we're hoping that her new tutor will make all the difference."

The other man nodded. After a few more moments of

comfortable silence, the master prompted him gently. "And yours?"

"Oh, they're well enough. I think Ronald is going to get into the college that he was hoping for. And Flo is almost over that dreadful bout of consumption, although the doctor believes she'll always be sickly." The man sighed. "Did you know that I had another son, long ago?"

The master looked surprised. "No, actually. All these years we've been friends, you've never mentioned it."

"It was always too painful even to think about," said the other man. "I haven't spoken of him for many years. Today would be his twentieth birthday. He's been on my mind all day."

"I'm so sorry, Joseph." The master shook his head. "What happened to him? The pox?"

"No. No, it would almost have been easier if I'd known he was dead." The man sighed heavily. "He just disappeared. Right out of his crib in the middle of the night – alongside his nurse. She must have stolen him. We searched through this entire city for him, but how do you find one small baby in a city of this size?" He shrugged helplessly. "He's just gone, and I'll never really know what happened to him."

Ivy grimaced in sympathy with the man. She'd finished mopping up the stain and straightened, balancing the tray on her hip, headed toward the door. She had almost reached it when she saw a flash of gold somewhere behind her – a familiar color, the exact hue of George's hair. She spun around, wanting to shout his name, to tell him to get out of here.

But George wasn't in the room. Instead, for the first time, the firelight had reflected off the hair of the thoughtful man sitting opposite her master. It was neatly kept and graying slightly, but apart from that, its brilliant color in the firelight was the exact same hue as George's.

She realized that she was staring when the man looked up at her. Giving a hurried little curtsy, she scurried out of the room, closing the door quietly behind her. But instead of rushing down to the kitchen, she leaned against the door for a minute, trying to stop her spinning world.

The man's eyes were a gentle brown. And they were as deep as seas.

"Phew," said Mildred, drawing a hand over her brow as she surveyed the giant pile of dishes that she and Ivy had just finished washing. "What a day."

"It was a long one, that's for sure," said Ivy.

"I'm ready to get into bed." Mildred leaned against the sink, blowing out a tired breath. Ivy noticed that there were dark circles underneath her friend's eyes. "I'm going to sleep like a baby."

Ivy glanced around the kitchen. They were alone, so she turned to Mildred. "I'll take George his supper," she said quietly.

"It's all right," said Mildred with a quick smile. "You did lunch. I'll sort out supper – you get to bed."

"No, really. You've done more than enough." Ivy gave Mildred a hug. "Get in bed – you're exhausted."

"If you're sure," said Mildred reluctantly.

"I'm completely sure." Ivy made a shooing motion with her hands. "Go."

Relieved, Mildred stumbled off. Ivy quickly gathered a few scraps together, adding a little of her own dinner, and made her way to George's room.

"Ivy." George looked both relieved and delighted when she came in. "I was starting to worry that you'd been found out."

"No, no." Ivy smiled. "It's just been a long day – like I warned you." She unwrapped the scrap of newspaper that she'd used to carry his dinner in. "Sorry. It's cold again."

"That's all right. I don't mind," said George quickly. He stared hungrily at the food that Ivy put down on his tray. "You look tired."

"I am a little tired," said Ivy. She sat down on the edge of his bed again. "At least tomorrow is Sunday, and I'll have a few hours off."

George bent his head, and Ivy stayed silent as he said grace. As soon as he was done, he seized the slice of cold meat she'd brought him and stuffed it whole into his mouth. Ivy watched him eat, relieved to see his appetite returning. She let him get halfway through his meal before speaking. "So," she said, as casually as she could. "What do you remember from... you know, when you were a little boy?"

George looked up in surprise. "What an odd thing to ask. Well, not much," he admitted. "Mostly just begging and singing on street corners, the same things I taught the children in my group. Nell taught me all of that." He smiled ruefully. "She wasn't quite as nice as your Aunt Bertha, though. Although, I guess she must have been better than my parents, considering that they didn't want me. I'm still not sure why she took me, if she didn't like me."

"Why didn't you leave?" Ivy asked softly.

"I was little," said George. "Staying with Nell seemed like a better option than being stuck on the streets alone. She was unkind, and she used me as a beggar because I got more sympathy from people than she did, but at least she gave me food." He sighed. "It was hard alone, at first, until I found the warehouse. I don't think I could have survived without it."

"You don't remember your parents at all?" asked Ivy, her heart hammering inside of her.

"No." George shook his head. "I only remember Nell. I don't know anything about them, except that I got this armband from them. Remember? I told you about it before." He shook it out of his sleeve and glanced at it. "I don't even really know why I've kept it all this time. Nell wanted to sell it a few times, but like I told you, I hid it from her." He shrugged. "I guess it's the only connection I have with my parents. I often wonder who they are. And why they didn't want me."

The pain in his voice tugged at Ivy's heart. She leaned over, laying her hand over his. The words came unbidden and suddenly. "I'm here," she said. "And I want you."

Their eyes locked, and Ivy saw the same gentleness in his expression that she'd seen in that of the man back in the parlor. Her heart thumped with sudden hope, but she knew she couldn't share it with George just yet.

Not until her suspicion became a fact.

CHAPTER 18

Ivy's arms and legs were so tired that it felt like her blood had been replaced with lead. She dragged herself into bed, barely bothering to kick off her shoes before pulling her blanket up to her chin. The mattress was thin and her bed so narrow that rolling over put her in serious danger of falling right onto the floor, but it had been hers for so long that she couldn't imagine sleeping better anywhere else.

But not tonight. She stared up at the ceiling, wide awake. Her mind was running circles, loud and insistent. Turning this way and that, she couldn't seem to get comfortable. It was as if her thoughts were too loud to let her go to sleep – a constant stream of "What if's?" pounding against the insides of her skull.

"Ivy," Mildred hissed, sitting up.

Ivy startled. She wasn't sure for how long she'd been tossing and turning. "Sorry," she whispered. "I didn't mean to wake you."

"What's going on?" Mildred asked, stifling a yawn. "Normally you go straight to sleep."

"It's nothing," said Ivy, not wanting to keep her friend out of her precious few hours of rest. "Go back to sleep."

"Really?" Mildred shook her head. "I've known you for years, Ivy, and this is the first time you've had trouble getting to sleep. And you expect me to believe that it's just nothing?"

Ivy sighed. "I'll tell you in the morning."

"Oh, so that we can both lie awake? No." Mildred crossed her arms. "What is it?"

Ivy sat up, pulling her blanket around her shoulders to stay warm. "Do you remember I told you how George's parents didn't want him and gave him to a woman who lived on the streets?"

"Yes, I do." Mildred's expression saddened. "I can't imagine why they'd do that to a little baby. I suppose they must have been hungry themselves."

"Well, what if they didn't give him away?" Ivy shivered a little. "What if he was taken?"

Mildred frowned. "What makes you say that?" she asked. "Isn't the lady who raised him dead already?"

"Yes – she has been for years. But... well, did you see the master's guest this evening?"

"No. I was in the kitchen all day." Mildred stared at Ivy. "What are you getting at?"

"I saw him. And Mildred..." Ivy's head was spinning, "he looked just like George – *exactly* like George. He had the same hair and eyes – even his voice sounded the same."

Mildred's expression grew softer. "Ivy," she said, gently. "You're tired. You've been nursing George almost non-stop for nearly a week. You're seeing things."

"I'm not," Ivy insisted. "And that's not all. I overheard him talking to the master, saying that he had a son that was taken away from him as a baby, stolen in the night by his nurse." She fixed her eyes on Mildred, willing her to understand. "The little boy would have been twenty years old today."

Momentarily, Mildred's eyes widened. "I suppose, then, that it's not impossible that this man could be..." She trailed off.

"He could be George's father," said Ivy.

The possibility hung in the air between them, big and brilliant. Mildred took a deep breath. "What are you going to do?"

"We can't tell George. Not yet," said Ivy. "If we're wrong, we could give him so much false hope. But we can't just leave it, either. If we're right..."

"It could change George's life," Mildred agreed. "We need to find out more before we do anything."

Ivy reached toward Mildred. Automatically, Mildred took Ivy's hand. Ivy gave it a squeeze. "Oh, Mildred, you've done so much for me," she said. "You're the best friend I've ever had. Can I ask you to do one more thing?"

"Of course, you can," said Mildred.

"Can you help me to find out more about that man who was here last night?"

"Of course." Mildred smiled in the darkness, her teeth glowing in the shadows. "We'll get to the bottom of this, Ivy. I'll do everything I can to help − I promise."

Ivy smiled. She knew that Mildred would stay true to her word.

☙❧

IVY COULD HARDLY BELIEVE THAT THE NEW LITTLE scullery-maid was the same age that she'd been when she'd first started working in the manor house. She looked so young; a little scrap of the girl, wide-eyed and bony. Fresh from the streets, she stared up at Ivy. "I'm so sorry, miss," she croaked, staring at the kitchen floor.

"It's all right," said Ivy, trying to smile, despite the fact that her heart had sunk into her feet the moment she'd walked through the door and seen the milk jug lying on the floor and milk absolutely everywhere. "I'll get it cleaned right up; don't you worry." She touched the girl's shoulder. "Mistakes happen – and it's no use crying over spilled milk, is it?"

The shadow of a smile crossed the girl's face. "No, miss."

"Good. Grab me that mop – let's get to it."

The milk seemed to have gone everywhere – under the table, under the sink, even into the tablecloth. Ivy and the girl mopped and scrubbed for what felt like hours before the floor was finally clean again. "There you go," Ivy said, wringing out the mop for a last time. "Good as new."

"Thank you for helping me, miss," said the girl, obviously relieved. "That was a lot of milk."

The kitchen door banged open. Both Ivy and the girl jumped, and Mildred charged inside. Her face was flushed, her eyes shining with uncharacteristic excitement.

"Ivy," she cried. "I have the most wonderful news."

Ivy stared at her for a minute, knowing that only one thing would get Mildred this excited. She turned to the girl, laying a hand on her shoulder. "We're going to need some more milk," she said. "I think the housekeeper is in the pantry right now, making a shopping list – go and tell her. Tell her that I spilled it, all right?" she added.

"Yes, miss. Thank you, miss." The girl scurried off.

Ivy looked up at Mildred. "What is it?" she asked.

"It's about the man that you think might be – you know, *his* father," said Mildred. She grabbed Ivy's shoulders. "I spoke to Bobby – he goes everywhere, delivering his papers, and he was able to find a few things out for me. The man's name is Joseph Shaw, and he lives not far from here. Just two streets down, Bobby said, in another big house. He's a merchant and travels a lot, but Bobby says he's home and probably will be for a few weeks."

"That's wonderful, Mildred." Ivy's heart was hammering. "What are we going to do?"

"What can we do?" Mildred shrugged. "We have to tell George. We have to get him to go there – the man might chase him off and break George's heart, but it's a risk that we have to take."

Ivy nodded slowly. "We'd have to smuggle him out of here again," she said. "It won't be easy."

"We got him in. We'll get him out," said Mildred. She handed Ivy a slip of paper. "Here, I had Bobby write down the address for me. Show it to George tonight and see if he recognizes it."

The kitchen door opened again, and Ivy hastily tucked the paper up her sleeve. The little scullery-maid hurried into the room.

"What is it?" asked Ivy.

"It's the young master," she said. "He wants someone to come and clean up some water that he spilled in his study."

"Well, it's quite the day for spilling things," said Ivy.

"I'll go," said Mildred.

"No, it's all right. I've got the mop ready," said Ivy, laughing. "A glass of water will be nothing after all the milk I've just cleaned up."

She emptied the dirty water out of the bucket and headed up the stairs, hauling the heavy wooden bucket along with her. The young master's study was all the way at the other end of the house, and she was breathless by the time she reached his door and knocked. "Come to clean your floor, sir," she said.

"Come in," came the voice from inside.

Ivy pushed the door open and carried her mop and bucket inside. The young master was sitting behind his desk, but this time he wasn't writing or studying. Instead, his eyes followed her inside. "Oh, it's you," he said, quietly. "I'd hoped it would be you."

Ivy's heart gave an unpleasant little thump. She swallowed, trying to dismiss the sudden fear rising in the back of her throat. "Where did you say you wanted me to clean up the water, sir?" she asked, keeping her eyes away from his.

The young master rose, walking toward the study door. He pushed it shut with a little click, then turned to Ivy, crossing the floor toward her in prowling steps. She clung to her bucket, feeling her hands begin to tremble.

"You're awfully pretty, for a kitchen maid," he purred.

Ivy refused to look at him. She stared down at the floor, acutely aware of how close he was. The smell of his cologne was suddenly the most repulsive thing ever to reach her senses.

"Sir?" she croaked.

"I've watched you grow up in this house." The young master's fingers hooked her hair out of her face, tucking it behind her ear. Her skin crawled where his fingertips touched her. "You were just a little thing when you arrived, but now... you've become quite the young lady." He moved closer, his hand sliding around the back of her neck.

Ivy pulled away, taking a quick step back. "Sir, please."

"Oh, don't play hard to get with me, girl." The young master's hand closed on her arm. "You're not going to be able to run very far." He yanked her closer, pulling her against him, and Ivy's body burned with panic.

"No!" she gasped, as the young master seized her other arm. The bucket clattered to the floor. "No! Let me go! HELP!"

The young master's eyes flashed. He grabbed her, spinning her against the wall, pinning her there with terrible strength. "Be quiet," he snarled.

"HELP!" Ivy screamed again. This time, the young master drew back his arm and gave her a ringing slap across the face. It burned, making stars pop in front of her eyes, but Ivy kept struggling. "Let me go!" she cried.

"Why, you little—" The young master's hand closed around Ivy's throat, and terror stabbed through her as she tried to take a breath and couldn't. She kicked, grasping madly at his hand, hearing her own breath gurgling in her throat, feeling the darkness gather at the corners of her vision...

There was a crash. The young master's hand slackened on Ivy's throat, and she took a gasping, struggling breath.

"What—" the young master began. Then there was a terrible thump, a crunch of bone on bone, and Ivy was free. She fell to her hands and knees, gasping for breath, and looked up.

The young master lay spread eagle on the floor, his chin tipped up, a bruise already swelling on his jaw. And standing over him, clutching his right hand in his left, was George. His golden hair blazed like a halo around his head, his brown eyes suddenly filled with fire and fury.

"George! How did you kn—" Ivy struggled to her feet and grabbed his arm. "You have to go! Get out of here!"

"Are you all right? I heard you scream. I wouldn't have heard, but Mildred had left my door open earlier. I'd gotten up to shut it and I heard from the stairwell..." George's eyes searched her, suddenly gentle again. "Did he harm you?"

"No. Go, George. Just go!"

But it was already too late. There were running feet in the hallway, and the master of the house appeared in the door. His expression went from shock to anger as he stared at George.

"What is this?" he roared, rushing into the room and seizing George by the arm. "Have you come in here to accost my maids and assault my son?"

"It's your son who was doing the accosting, sir," George spat, fearlessly raising his chin to glare into the master's eyes.

The master's eyes widened. "How dare you accuse my son of such a thing?" he bellowed. "Who are you? How did you get into my house?"

Ivy saw him freeze. The master's glare intensified as he looked George up and down, taking in his dirty feet and ragged clothes.

"Did you break in?" he demanded. "My son must have tried to stop you robbing the place. You thief!"

"No!" Ivy couldn't bear it. She rushed up to the master, grasping George's hand on her way. "He's not a thief. He never has been."

"Ivy, hush!" snapped George.

"I won't." Ivy trembled, staring at the master, trying to keep down her fear. "George is an old friend of mine," she said. "He was hurt, so I brought him here."

"You..." The master's expression went wild with rage. "You smuggled a young man into my household?"

Ivy swallowed. "Yes," she whispered.

The master drew himself up, and Ivy cowered, expecting a slap. Instead, he glanced at George's expression and seemed to think better of it.

"Get out of my house," he hissed at them both. "Get out of my house and never, ever come back here." He pointed a trembling finger, toward the exit. "Get away from here. You are dismissed!"

CHAPTER 19

Ivy had never seen Mildred cry before. It was a shock to see the tears streaming down her best friend's face as she stood in the doorway, sniffing, trying to wipe them away.

"Oh, Ivy," she whispered. "I can't believe you're going."

"It's all right, Mildred." Ivy took her friend's hands. "I didn't let the master know you were part of any of it. You're safe."

"I don't care about that right now." Mildred looked up at Ivy through her tears. "What are you going to do?"

Ivy looked back. George stood on the path a few yards away, resting his injured leg, but smiling. Her heart skipped a beat.

"I'm going to the warehouse with George," she told Mildred gently. "It's all right. I'll be safe. It'll all be all right — you'll see."

"I'm going to miss you so much." Mildred swallowed, gulping at her tears. "What will I do without you? You're my best friend."

"And you're mine." Ivy put her arms around Mildred and hugged her tightly, feeling tears gather in her throat. "You can come see me, all right? On Sundays. I'll miss you, too." She swallowed hard. "Thank you for everything."

"Thank you, too." Mildred pulled back, wiping at her tears. "The master will be angry if you stay here for too long. You – you had better go."

Suddenly, Ivy didn't want to leave. She squeezed Mildred's hands. "All right. I'll see you again."

"I'll see you soon," said Mildred hopefully, plastering a brave smile over her face. Ivy picked up the bag that contained everything she owned in the world – a few coins, a book she'd bought with months of saving up, and a spare dress. She gave Mildred one last smile, then reached for George's hand and held it tightly as he limped up the path and onto the street.

STROLLING THROUGH THE STREETS WITH GEORGE FELT strange and lovely, especially with his hand steadily holding hers. They had to walk slowly to allow for his wounded leg, but it was healing well, and he seemed to manage without too much effort as they moved through the streets.

FAYE GODWIN

"You know," Ivy said, "just after I left the warehouse for the first time, I came looking for you every Sunday."

George glanced at her. "You did?"

"Yes. I came and watched you every week." Ivy smiled. "It was the only thing that kept me going before Mildred and I really became friends."

"Why did you never come up to me?" George's voice was wounded. "I was desperate to find you."

"I believed that I was nothing but a burden on you and the rest of the group." Ivy looked away. "I didn't want to hurt you."

"Oh, Ivy." George squeezed her hand. "Staying away hurt me more than anything else you could have done."

She swallowed. "Can you ever forgive me?"

They had reached the street where his new warehouse was, and George stopped, turning to her. He laid his hands on her shoulders, pulling her closer and kissing her forehead. The touch of his lips on her skin made her heart thunder.

"I already forgave you long ago," he whispered. "I'm just glad you're back." His eyes shone. "Never do that to me again, all right?"

"Never," Ivy whispered back.

"George!"

Joan's high voice filled the entire street. Ivy turned. Joan was standing in the warehouse door, her eyes wide, hands clapped over her mouth. She allowed her thin arms to fall by her sides and turned back, shouting into the warehouse.

"It's George," she cried. "It's George! He's back. He's not dead!"

Excited, high-pitched voices clamored in the warehouse, and the next thing Ivy knew, a sea of children was rushing toward them. Their arms were waving, eyes wide and adoring as they rushed toward George. He limped forward, letting go of Ivy's hand, his face transfixed with joy.

"Oh, Joan! Gordon! I missed you all so much. Come here!" He held out his arms and was swamped by the crowd of children. They threw their arms around him, clambered up him to sit on his shoulders, clutched at his hair, shouted with joy as they grasped his hands and arms.

Ivy couldn't stop smiling as she watched. She couldn't imagine how much these little children had missed him. Covered in a happy tangle of young limbs, George was exactly where he belonged – protecting the group of people that he loved.

"Is he well again?" The voice beside Ivy startled her. She jumped, looking around. Jane was standing right next to her, and there was something venomous in her eyes that made Ivy's stomach clench with fear. "Why are you back so soon? He's still pale."

"He's getting better," said Ivy, trying to soothe her own jangled nerves. "I would have liked for him to stay a little longer, but the master of the house found us out. He dismissed me."

"So, you thought you would come back here with him?" Jane crossed her arms. "The only reason I involved you in the first place was because I knew he'd have a better chance at that house. Be warmer and better fed. And I was desperate. But you're crazy if you think you're going to pick up where you left off after you disappeared into thin air years ago."

Ivy felt a cold rush of anger. She raised her chin. "I didn't just disappear, Jane," she said. "You threw me out."

"And why do you think I did that?" asked Jane, her voice icy. "You were nothing to the group." She took a step closer, reminding Ivy how much taller she was. "You don't belong here."

Ivy laughed, shaking her head. "It's not going to work this time. George asked me to stay. George *wants* me to stay."

She saw pain turn to fury in Jane's eyes. "You're a thief and a liar."

"Maybe I am," said Ivy, "but that doesn't change the fact that I'm here now, and George wants me here. I'm staying, Jane. You're not going to throw me out this time."

Jane's voice remained a low hiss, as furious as it was quiet.

"Very well," she said. "If you feel that way, then stay." She took a step back. "But I'll turn George in to the police."

Ivy felt as though all her blood had suddenly turned to ice. She gaped for a moment, unable to get a word out. "What?" she croaked.

"You heard me," said Jane. Her eyes were ablaze with fury. "I'll tell the police that he's the leader of a gang of criminals."

Ivy knew that they had no way of proving that the stockpiled food hadn't been stolen. "But they'll put him in prison." She gasped. "And all the children will go to the workhouse. You can't do that, Jane."

"It's better than having *you* here," Jane snapped. "I'll do it, Ivy. I'll go right now, and your precious George will rot in jail."

Ivy stared at her. "Why do you hate me so much?" she whispered. "Why would you have George thrown in jail if you're so jealous of me?"

Jane didn't respond. "Make your choice," she spat.

Ivy looked over at George. He had one of the smaller children on his shoulders, and he was laughing with joy. Ivy couldn't hurt him. She couldn't do anything to hurt him – not now or ever.

"All right," she heard herself say. "Fine. I'm going."

CHAPTER 20

Ivy had almost forgotten how cold the nights were out on the streets. She pulled her coat as tightly around her shoulders as she could, stumbling through the twilight, her eyes scanning every nook and cranny she passed. She'd long since cut up her bag to make herself an extra pair of socks the way that Bertha had taught her. Now, she clutched a hunk of cold, hard cheese in one hand, two copper pennies in the other. It was all that she had left of the money she'd saved, and she knew it wouldn't feed her for long.

She didn't allow herself to think about what she'd do when the money ran out. She just thought of where she was going to sleep tonight. Every alley seemed to be occupied by rough-looking men and women who glared at her as she passed, daring her to trespass on their territory. There seemed to be dogs chained up in all the doorways, snarling at her.

It was pitch dark by the time Ivy found an alley that seemed empty but for a barrel that was missing some planks from its sides. Numb with cold, Ivy crawled inside. She kept her money tightly in her hand as she started to eat the cheese in small bites, trying her best to make it last for as long as possible. Maybe she'd feel less hungry that way. It didn't seem to help; in what felt like a few seconds, the cheese was gone.

Ivy sighed, making herself as comfortable as she could in the barrel. She stared through one of the holes in its side, gazing at the stars beyond the washed-out glow of the nearby lamp-post. Was George looking at these same stars? Was he heart-broken? Was he looking for her? She couldn't run the risk of letting Jane go to the police, that much she knew. But she also knew that what she'd done had hurt him. Closing her eyes, she allowed her pain to carry her off into a painful sleep.

There was a loud crack. Ivy gasped to wakefulness, throwing out her arms and legs as her whole world seemed to be spin-ning. It *was* spinning – the barrel was rolling, tossing her around inside, slamming her painfully this way and that. It came to a halt with a bump, and Ivy fell to the ground, gasping in fear and pain.

"Get her out of there," growled a rough voice. Ivy cowered, but it was no good. The barrel was seized and turned upside down, and she tumbled out onto the floor.

Looking up, she saw two men glaring down at her. Their beards and hair were wild, and a filthy stench rolling off them.

Ivy scrambled to her feet, acutely aware of the cold, hard shapes of the pennies in her fist.

"What have you got there, little lady?" sneered one of them, taking a step closer. His eyes were wild.

Ivy hid her hand behind her back, saying nothing.

"Oh, so it *is* something." His sneer widened. "Get it."

The other man, taller and more muscular, lurched forward. Ivy tried to bolt, ducking under his arm and rushing for the entrance of the alley, but a swift kick to her shins brought her crashing to the floor. The pennies slid out of her hand, and she watched them skitter off across the dirt. They were snatched up in a moment, and the man grinned triumphantly. "Got any more where that came from, little missy?" he hissed.

"No," Ivy choked out, trying to get up. This time, the tall man's boot thudded into her stomach. She curled up, agony filling her, tears prickling at her eyes. "I don't have anything left!" she screamed. "I have nothing left. I have nothing!"

The tall man grabbed her arm, yanking her to her feet, and desperation filled Ivy's mind. She lashed out, raking her fingernails down the side of his face. With a yowl, he flinched back, his hand opening on her arm, and Ivy saw her chance. Despite the pain in her stomach and shins, she bolted out of the alleyway and into the street as fast as her legs could carry her.

"OH, MA'AM," IVY SAID, STRETCHING HER EYES AS WIDE AS they could go. "I'm s-s-so sorry about what happened last week." She sniffed, allowing a tear to run down her cheek. "It – it was all so horrible. I was just walking on the street, and that terrible man came out of nowhere. He grabbed me and put a knife to my throat." She sobbed, covering her face with her hands. "He said he'd kill me if I didn't help him with his leg. I tried to tell the young master what happened, but before I could do anything, that awful man was there. He was going to kill me, ma'am. I d-d-didn't know what to d-d-do."

She lifted her face from her hands and looked up hopefully. Swaying serenely in the breeze, the bare branches of the elm tree on the corner of the street gave her no reply. Quickly wiping away her tears, Ivy swallowed.

"No," she murmured to herself. "That won't work. The young master knows I didn't try to tell him anything. I'll have to tell her that George followed me up to the study, wanting to rob the young master."

Her own words hurt, but she pushed the pain aside until it was only a dull throb. She knew she could never even imagine George doing such a thing and saying it out loud – even to herself – felt like a betrayal. She sighed, sitting on the pavement around the corner from the manor house. Rehearsing the lies she'd tell the housekeeper to get her position back hurt badly enough that she knew actually telling – and then living – them would be agony, but what choice did she have?

Eating is a good thing, she thought, looking down at her empty hands. It had been days since she'd last eaten anything. She had no choice.

Getting up from the street corner, she limped down the street. The manor house was just up ahead, and the sight of it made Ivy want to run forward and laugh with joy. There was a warm fire inside, she knew, and plenty of food, and even Mildred's smile to lift her spirits. Everything was going to be just fine. She just had to tell one more little lie, and she would be safe again.

She reached the servant's entrance and took a deep breath, running her story through her head one more time, just the same way as Bertha had taught her. She raised her hand to knock. And she froze.

Stealing's not a good thing, but eating is a good thing, and if we want to keep eating, we have to keep stealing. She closed her eyes, forcing herself to remember Bertha's voice. She was right. She had to do what she had to do to survive. It was this or die out here on the streets. She raised her hand again but stopped before her knuckles could meet the wood.

She remembered Bertha lying in the back of that filthy warehouse, her life slowly slipping away. Her eyes had been as warm as ever, her voice cracked and struggling. *You keep looking for the light,* she'd said. *Keep looking for the light.*

Ivy closed her eyes. The light. It had been the last thing on Bertha's mind before she died, the only thing to bring her peace as the life drained out of her. Ivy tried to think of light, somewhere in her struggles, after Bertha's death. And she thought of golden light, glowing, shining strands of light falling around George's face, pouring out of his eyes as he smiled, filling his touch as he reached for her, filling her soul as he kissed her forehead.

She opened her eyes. The thought of walking away made everything inside her tremble.

You be brave, she heard her aunt's voice say. *You be brave.*

"I am brave," Ivy whispered.

Then she turned around and walked slowly back into the cold and empty street.

CHAPTER 21

When Ivy opened the lid of the refuse bin, the smell that blossomed out of its nauseating depths made her empty stomach churn. She heaved but knew that nothing would come of it; she had nothing left inside her. She couldn't remember the last time she'd eaten. Peering into the refuse bin, she waited for her eyes to adjust to the gloom inside. Maybe there would be something in there – something apart from whatever it was that gave off that appalling stench, anyway. A crust of bread or an apple core. Her stomach growled. At this point, she'd take anything.

She was moving aside a scrap of dirty newspaper when she heard the yell. "You! You there!"

Tiredly, Ivy replaced the lid of the dustbin and looked up. A man was standing on the steps of the cottage nearby, his hands planted on his hips.

"Get away from there!" he yelled, waving his hand to shoo her off. "I'll set the dogs on you! Get away!"

Ivy would have run if she'd had the strength. Instead, she turned around and staggered off, her heart so heavy that she felt like it might drop out of her chest and land with a clang on the street. Struggling to keep her eyes open, she staggered along until she found a patch of sunshine on the walkway. Her legs wouldn't go any further. She sat down heavily, pulled up her knees, and rested her forehead on them. She was so tired, but the pangs in her stomach wouldn't let her sleep.

At least the sunshine was quite nice. It caressed the back of her neck, warming the bruises that covered her arms and legs, and it found its way through the rips in her dress. Ivy knew someone would be along to chase her off soon, but for now, she enjoyed the bit of warmth. Her eyes closed, and her thoughts drifted off to George, as they always did. He was safe and happy in the warehouse, playing with the children, teaching them new things. They'd be on their way back to their home now, ready for supper and a round of games before sleeping on their little pallets, and George would be worrying about them the way he always did, but he would gaze at their sleeping little faces, and he would be happy.

She could hear them now, chattering away to him, telling him all about their day and what they hoped to do tomorrow or singing him songs they had perfected. She could almost hear his name spoken nearby, and it sent a lance of light into her aching heart. *George*.

Ivy looked up, startled. It had really sounded as if someone was talking about him nearby. She blinked and rubbed her eyes. The hunger must have gone to her head, she thought.

Then she saw them. Two small children, a boy and a girl, whose faces looked familiar. They were walking up the street hand-in-hand.

"George will be so happy with all the coins we got today," the girl was saying in excitement. "We'll be able to buy lots of bread with it, don't you think?"

"Yes, we will," said the boy happily. "He was right about the new song that he gave us – it's made lots more money than the old one today."

The little girl sighed, looking up at the boy. "Do you think it'll make him happy for a bit?" she asked. "He's been so sad ever since he got back and Ivy left. He loved her so much. He couldn't believe she left again."

"I hope so," said the little boy solemnly. "I heard people can die from a broken heart."

"Do you think George will die?" asked the girl, frightened.

"Let's hope not." The boy put his arm around her shoulders, and they turned onto a side street and disappeared.

Ivy stared after them. Her heart felt like it had been ripped out of her chest and stomped on. George wasn't content and happy – he was heartbroken, depressed, and it was all because of her. She'd left him and broken the last promise she'd ever made to him, and it was killing him.

"Oh, George." Ivy buried her face in her hands, feeling tears fill her eyes and nose. "I did it to protect you."

George didn't know that. And she could never go back and tell him. She pushed her hands into the pockets of her dress, searching for something to wipe away her tears, and found a scrunched-up little ball of paper. Lifting it out, she was about to wipe her eyes with it when she saw the writing.

It was Mildred's handwriting. *Joseph Shaw*, it said, followed by an address.

Ivy's heart thumped. Joseph Shaw – the man who might be George's father. She'd been too scared to go to him before now; without George, he would never have believed her. But what did it matter now? What more could he do to her than had already been done?

Ivy rose to her feet, reading the address again. She could never go to be with George again. But maybe – it was a gamble, but maybe – she could still help him in one last way.

SHAW MANOR WAS ENORMOUS, BIGGER EVEN THAN THE house where Ivy and Mildred had worked together. Ivy stared up at its tall palisade gates. They towered into the sky, their pointy tips seeming to spear the setting sun. It looked as impregnable as any fortress, and for a moment, her heart sank.

She sagged onto the pavement beside the gates, peering through the fence at the house at the top of the hill. It was surrounded by a green, landscaped lawn. Ivy pictured baby George sitting on the lawn, giggling as he played. She wondered what his childhood would have been like, assuming he really was Joseph Shaw's son. Playing on the lawn, learning his lessons inside the vaulted hallways of that enormous house – it would have been perfect. And she would have died, alone and scared, beside Bertha's corpse.

One thing was for sure: getting through those gates would be impossible. Ivy would have to wait until Joseph Shaw came out – and hopefully he would do that soon. Her hands trembled with weakness. She laid them on her knees to steady them and gazed through the fence, waiting for the gates to open. Her head slowly nodded forward onto her chest.

The next thing Ivy knew was the sound of clattering hoofbeats. Gasping to wakefulness, she scrambled to her feet. In the light of the lamps on the pillars of the gates, she saw a four-horse coach charging down the drive, sparks flying from the hooves of the horses. The coach skidded to a halt, and a footman jumped down and ran to open the gates.

The moment they opened, Ivy ran in front of the coach. Steam rolled from the horses' nostrils; they startled, skittering away from her, and the coachman shouted angrily at them. Ivy ignored them. She stared desperately into the coach's dark interior.

"Joseph Shaw!" she cried. "Joseph Shaw!"

"Who is it, Larson?" The voice from inside the coach was so familiar that, for a moment, Ivy thought it was George.

"Some homeless woman, sir," said the coachman, angrily reining the horses in.

"Get past her," said the voice in irritation. "I'm in a hurry."

"Go on!" The coachman cracked his whip threateningly, making the horses jump forward. "Get out of here!"

"Joseph Shaw!" Ivy shouted.

"Get!" The coachman snapped the whip and the horses leaped forward again. Ivy could smell their sweaty flanks, feel their hot breath on her face, but she didn't move. "Joseph Shaw!" she yelled. "Joseph Shaw, I know your son, George!"

"STOP!" Mr. Shaw's voice was final and thunderous.

The coachman yanked on the reins, and the horses skidded to a halt. One of them huffed in Ivy's face. She looked up as Mr. Shaw leaned out of the window, his golden hair gleaming in the lantern light. His eyes were wide, yet suspicious. "How do you know my lost boy's name?" he demanded. "Nobody outside the family knows that."

"Mr. Shaw, I know your son," Ivy repeated, stepping toward him. "He calls himself George Taylor. He looks just like you."

Mr. Shaw stared at her. There was a moment's silence. "The nurse that kidnapped my son was named Taylor," he said, his voice quaking. "Who are you?"

"I'm nobody," said Ivy. "But I know him."

"How would you know him?" asked Mr. Shaw.

The truth spilled out of Ivy from somewhere deep in her soul. "I lived with my aunt, and we were thieves and beggars," she told him. "But when my auntie died, I had nowhere to go. It was George who found me and saved me. He lives in a warehouse with a gang of children that he takes care of, but they never steal. They only beg or sing and dance on street corners. George is brave and noble and strong and..." Ivy swallowed, suddenly choked with tears. "He deserves a better life than the one he has. He deserves to be your son."

There were tears gleaming in Mr. Shaw's eyes. Ivy went on. "I'm just a thief and a beggar, Mr. Shaw. But I know your boy, and I would do anything for him – anything in the whole world. Please, let me take you to him."

The coachman shook his head. "Looks suspicious, sir," he grunted.

Mr. Shaw didn't look at him. His eyes were fixed on Ivy. "Get in the carriage," he said. "Take me to my son."

CHAPTER 22

Ivy could tell that Mr. Shaw was repulsed by the interior of the warehouse. Its fatty stench was appalling even to her; he had taken his handkerchief out and held it over his nose and mouth as he followed her deeper into the guts of the place.

"This place is reprehensible," he muttered, giving Ivy a suspicious glance. "Maybe I shouldn't have followed you in here after all."

"We're almost there, sir," said Ivy. She felt as if she were floating now, as if her body was barely able to keep a tenuous grip on her mind. They wound their way between heaps of junk until they saw the flicker of firelight against the walls. Ivy knew they were close, and her heart hammered. What if she was wrong? Would Jane still turn George in to the police if she spotted Ivy? Would Mr. Shaw lose his nerve or discover that George wasn't his son?

They detoured around a stack of rubbish, and then George was there, right in front of them. He was standing by the fire, telling the children a story, his hands held high as he brought his tale to life. "And then," he said, "the prince came riding out of the woods, and—"

"George?" Mr. Shaw whispered.

George whipped around. His golden hair bounced in the fire-light, and when he saw Mr. Shaw, his eyes widened in fear.

"Jane!" he shouted. "Get the children out of here. Go!"

The children began to scurry around, and George stepped forward, his hands balled into fists. Ivy saw the fire in his eyes again, the same fire that had saved her from the young master.

"I don't know who you are," he said, his voice shaking, "but you won't lay a finger on them."

"I'm not here to hurt you, George," said Mr. Shaw. He took a step nearer, his eyes searching. "You – you look just like me. Just like when you were a baby."

George's face filled with confusion, but the set of his shoulders was stiff and wary. "What do you want?" he demanded. "Who are you?"

Mr. Shaw kept coming closer, his voice still trembling. "You –

you were so young," he whispered. "You won't remember. Of course, you wouldn't." Ivy could hear tears in his voice. "But I remember. I never forgot you. Not for one moment."

He was standing only inches from George now, who seemed frozen to the spot, staring at the man who might be his father.

"Who are you?" George demanded.

In response, Mr. Shaw reached for George's arm. The younger man drew back, but Mr. Shaw's touch was gently insistent. He took George's wrist and pushed back the sleeve of his ragged shirt. The brass of the armband gleamed in the firelight, and Mr. Shaw's shoulders sagged with something that groaned out of him like the roar of a bear. And then it looked as if he might slump to the ground, he began shaking so visibly.

"Oh, George," he moaned, shaking back the well-cut sleeve of his own jacket to show an identical band on his own arm. "I'm your father."

George's eyes widened. He stared from his own band to his father's, and his mouth opened and shut a few times with no sound coming out.

"But... but..." he managed at last. "You didn't want me. You gave me away."

"No, George, *no*." Mr. Shaw laid his hands on George's shoulders. "I would never have done that. I loved you. *We* loved you. Your nurse... Curse the woman! Where is she anyway?

Nell Taylor stole you from us, and we never stopped searching for you."

Tears were running down the older man's cheeks now.

"We never stopped searching," he repeated.

George's own eyes were filled with tears now as the other children, who hadn't yet escaped, all stared in amazement.

"Oh." George looked stupefied. Ivy feared he might faint, but he didn't.

"Oh... Papa!" he cried and threw his arms around his father and clung to him, his body racked with sobs.

Mr. Shaw fiercely embraced his son for the first time in almost two decades, and his own shoulders were shaking.

"Hush," he whispered, clinging to George. "Hush now. It's all right. I'm here now."

"And... and Mama?" George choked out.

"She's at home. She, she won't believe this." Mr. Shaw's voice completely broke now and he sobbed as he continued to embrace George.

In the shadows of the rubbish surrounding them, Ivy began to weep. Then she spotted Jane on the edge of the group and knew that her moment of joy had ended. It was time to go. She was slipping away when George spoke again.

"How – how did you find me?" he asked.

"Oh, where is she?" Mr. Shaw backed away from George and turned around, and his eyes found Ivy. He pointed. "There – that girl. She said she knew you. She brought me here."

Ivy took another step back, but she wasn't quick enough. George crossed the distance between them in what seemed like two long bounds. He grabbed her arms, his eyes shining with joy, his cheeks with tears. "Oh no, you don't," he said, his hands trembling on her arms. "You're not going anywhere. I'll never, *ever* lose you again."

Ivy stared up at him, shaking with joy at his touch. "George," was all that she could manage.

"Don't even try to escape," he said. "I'm never letting you go."

It was the most natural thing in the world to throw her arms around him. And when he held her, the fervor of his embrace told her that he meant every word.

Ivy felt small and filthy in the courtyard of the manor house. She wondered if anything as dirty as she had ever been allowed this close to the gilded doors that towered before her, elegantly decorated with a lion's head knocker and polished brass studs. She knew she both smelled and looked worse than the lowliest scullery-maid in the entire manor, yet here she was, waiting just outside the main doors.

Mr. Shaw had told her that it was best to wait out here, which she understood. She was a street rat, after all; there was no lucky blood in her own veins waiting to call her back to a better life. It was fine with her. If she could just be a servant in their house, she would be quite content. It was enough to know that George was safe and happy.

The doors creaked, then swung open. Ivy got up, folding her hands as neatly as possible in her lap. She was painfully aware of how dirty her skin was, how ragged her dress. The woman standing in the doorway had George's snub nose and high cheekbones. Ivy felt her eyes travel from her bare feet to her filthy, torn dress, up to her tangled hair, and she could see the disgust and disapproval in the woman's face.

"Gertrude." Mr. Shaw appeared behind her, laying his hands on her shoulders. "This is Ivy."

Mrs. Shaw stared at Ivy for a long time. Ivy didn't dare look up to where George was waiting behind his parents.

Then, Mrs. Shaw's stern face crumpled. Tears filled her eyes, and she rushed forward, throwing her arms around Ivy's neck. Her satin dress pressed against Ivy's filthy body.

"Oh, Ivy," she choked out, sobs shaking her body. "Thank you. Thank you for saving my boy. Thank you for bringing my baby back to me."

Ivy didn't know whether she could hug Mrs. Shaw back, so she just stood there, letting the shock ripple through her.

"He saved me first," she said.

CHAPTER 23

Ivy remembered when she'd been paid to polish silver spoons like this one. She stirred her tea, staring thoughtfully into it. She'd been polishing spoons the day that Jane had come to the door of the manor house where she'd worked, telling her that George was dying.

How much had changed since then.

"Ivy? Are you listening?"

Ivy looked up. Mildred sat across from her, an eyebrow raised, holding her own teacup.

"Sorry, Mildred." Ivy smiled. "I was just thinking of old times."

"Oh, don't let's do that," said Mildred, shuddering. "I hate to think of my days as a kitchen maid working for my mother. My life has been so much better since you got me the housekeeping job at Shaw Manor. Mr. Shaw is a very kind master."

"And I'm sure you're much kinder to your kitchen maids than your mother was," said Ivy, with a wink.

"Oh no." Mildred laughed. "I terrorize the little things. They're very frightened of me." Her laugh bubbled, and Ivy leaned back in her comfortable chair, laughing with her. The summer sunlight filled her little flat, warming the nook by the bay window where she and Mildred had already drunk innumerable cups of tea together.

"You're right, Mildred," said Ivy, settling a little deeper into her chair. "It doesn't do to dwell on the past. Only a year ago, I was starving out on the street. And now, look at all this." She gestured at the room around them. "Mr. and Mrs. Shaw were so wonderful to set me up in my own little flat – I still can hardly believe it. They've provided everything I could have wanted."

"It's the least they can do," said Mildred. "You saved their son's life, after all. And you brought them back to him."

Ivy smiled. "You helped. If you hadn't written down that address for me, none of this ever would have happened."

Mildred laughed. "Let's call it a team effort." She swallowed the last of her tea. "Well, I had better get back to the manor. I've done the shopping for a dinner party tonight, and it needs to be cooked now." She winked. "Time to go and bully some little kitchen maids."

"Mildred," Ivy giggled. "Remember that some of those little kitchen maids are George's children. I think he's found positions for them all now. I'll see you tomorrow?"

"Probably," said Mildred, grinning. "What would I do without a daily dose of your tea?"

Ivy showed her friend out of her flat. She waved as Mildred reached the end of the street, then went back inside, heading toward one of the bookshelves that lined the walls. Dickens had just put out a new novel, and she couldn't wait to settle down with it. She pulled out the book and cracked it open, breathing the wonderful scent of ink and paper.

"Thank you, Auntie," she whispered. She remembered how Bertha had told her that reading might be the way to a better life. "I wish you could have had this life with me," she murmured.

There was a knock at the door, and Ivy's heart skipped a beat. Putting the book down on the nearest table, she hurried to the door and pulled it open. As she'd expected, George stood on the doorstep, a bunch of white roses in his hand.

"Oh!" she cried, smelling them. "They're beautiful!"

"Hello to you, too," said George, laughing, as he handed her the flowers. He kissed her forehead. "How are you today?"

"All the better now that you're here." Ivy gazed up at him, clutching the flowers to her chest.

"Always glad to brighten up your day."

"You always do." Ivy stood on tiptoe to give him a peck on the cheek. "Would you like some tea?"

"Yes, please," said George.

"Have a seat. I'll just put these in a vase."

Ivy arranged the roses in a pretty, pink vase and set them on the small table by the bay window before brewing another pot of tea for them both. She sat down beside George on the settee and handed him a cup.

"How are your studies going?" she asked.

"They're going well." George smiled. "My tutor says that I've caught up nicely, considering that I've only been able to have lessons for a year. Hopefully, I can still be a doctor someday."

"You've always dreamed of it," said Ivy, resting her hand in her lap.

"I have." George took a sip of his tea. He seemed a little nervous, replacing the cup in its saucer and putting it back on the table. He ran a finger inside his shirt collar and looked at Ivy with an awkward smile. "So, ah, any more luck thinking about what you would want to study?"

"Not yet." Ivy smiled up at him. "I still only know one thing — that I want to help street children. It's my biggest dream."

George took her hand, and his eyes became so intense that they took Ivy's breath away. "Then we can achieve that dream together," he whispered.

Ivy stared at him. "George?"

Slowly, George got up from the settee and lowered himself to one knee. Reaching into his coat pocket, he took out something that gleamed like gold, the same shade as his neatly cut and combed hair.

"George?" Ivy squeaked.

"Ivy Harris." George cleared his throat. "Would you do me the honor of being my wife?"

Ivy didn't know if she should laugh, cry, or jump up and down. She clung to his hand instead, her whole body trembling.

"Oh, George," she cried. "Do you even have to ask?"

And as George slid the ring onto her finger, Ivy could feel it all falling away — the cold, the hunger, the darkness, the loneliness, the cruel memories. All the dismay of her past, melted away, letting her go and disappearing somewhere so distant that it could never, ever come back.

Only the memories of her dear, dear auntie remained.

EPILOGUE

Ivy stirred the ladle around in the gigantic pot of soup that was bubbling on the huge coal stove that they'd installed in the corner of the warehouse. She scooped up some of the rich broth and spooned it into a bowl, then turned toward the small child standing by her side. The little girl's body was still pink from the good scrubbing that Ivy had just given her, her wet hair streaming over her shoulders, and her eyes widened as she took the bowl from Ivy.

"Golly, miss," she said. "That's a lot of soup."

"It certainly is," said Ivy, smiling as she handed the little girl a spoon. "And there's plenty more where that came from."

"Thanks, miss." The little girl scampered off to join the groups of children that sat at the long tables that were set out in rows down the length of the first floor of the warehouse.

Ivy stirred the soup absently, gazing at the many children who were filling their bellies and chattering away. She could remember so clearly how this warehouse had looked when it was still filled with old fabric rolls and other paraphernalia, when the floor was still coated in grime. Now, the first floor was one enormous kitchen, and above, she could hear the voice of one of their tutors giving a group of children their lesson.

It was in this very warehouse that Ivy had met George for the first time.

His arms gave her a little fright as he hugged her from behind.

"Oh, George!" she said, laughing. George kissed the back of her neck. She leaned against him, smiling. "You scared me."

"It's good to know that I can still do that, ten years into our marriage," said George. His voice rumbled pleasantly through him as Ivy leaned on him.

"How is the little sick one doing?" Ivy asked.

"She'll be just fine. Only a touch of cold, luckily," said George.

Ivy turned to him, putting her arms around his neck. She gazed into his brown eyes, loving every inch of him.

"I'm so proud of you," she said. "You're making such a difference in so many lives with this place."

George kissed her forehead. "It's all because of your courage," he said.

Ivy leaned against her husband, feeling his heartbeat against her skin, and her heart was filled with overwhelming gratitude. Gratitude for the first person who had ever told her to be brave. Gratitude for the woman whose name was written in big letters on the sign above the door: *Bertha Harris Children's Home*.

The End

CONTINUE READING...

Thank you for reading **Thief Girl! Are you wondering what to read next?** Why not read **A Daughter's Desperation? Here's a sneak peek for you:**

The sounds of the marketplace were so loud that Elsie could barely hear the vendor at the bakery stall. She leaned in a little closer, trying to concentrate as well as she could, but the noise around her was chaotic and distracting. Voices of all kinds haggled and shouted and laughed, children's footsteps slapped on the cobblestones, hoofbeats and squeaking carriage wheels traveled down the road, and dogs barked— even chickens squawked at one market stall. This place was a marvel, one of the rare spots near Elsie's slum where farmers could still set up stands in order to sell their wares cheaply.

"Sixpence?" Elsie asked, looking up at the baker as he loomed over her.

"To you, yes." He looked her up and down, with a sneer crinkling his lip.

Elsie was suddenly acutely aware of her dirty dress and scuffed shoes. She leaned forward a tiny bit, hoping that the ragged hem of her dress would hide the fact that her socks were mismatched and riddled with holes. Mother had told her to negotiate, and she tried to be brave as she stared up at the baker's mean eyes.

"Four pennies," she said, swallowing. "And not a farthing more."

The baker snorted, stepping back. "Don't waste my time," he spat. "Get out of my sight."

"No – please, please." Elsie stepped forward, almost dropping the coins she had clutched in her hand. "Please, it's all right. I-I have the money right here."

The baker moved back, still sneering at her. Elsie scraped together all the courage she could find, thinking of how far the money in her hand had to stretch.

"Five pence," she croaked, trying not to sound as terrified as she was.

The baker studied her for a few seconds, then shrugged. "Very well."

He watched Elsie slowly count the coins onto the front of his market stall, and only after he had carefully inspected each coin did he turn to the baskets of bread behind him. Elsie could feel her mouth water as the baker looked through the loaves of yesterday's bread in the baskets, finally selecting the smallest one before he turned back to her and slapped it carelessly onto the counter.

"Thank you," Elsie said. She grabbed the bread in both hands; it felt real and solid, and she couldn't wait to feel its reassuring weight in her stomach. She brought it close to her face and took a deep breath. It was a little stale, but to her starving senses, it still smelled wonderful.

"Push off," snapped the baker. "You're chasing away customers with your dirty face."

Visit Here to Continue Reading:

http://www.ticahousepublishing.com/victorian-romance.html

THANKS FOR READING

If you **love Victorian Romance**, <u>**Visit Here:**</u>

https://victorian.subscribemenow.com/

to hear about all <u>**New Faye Godwin Romance Releases! I will let you know as soon as they become available!**</u>

Thank you, Friends! If you enjoyed ***Thief Girl!*** would you kindly take a couple minutes to leave a positive review on Amazon? It only takes a moment, and positive reviews truly make a difference. Thank you so much! I appreciate it!

Much love,

Faye Godwin

ABOUT THE AUTHOR

Faye Godwin has been fascinated with Victorian Romance since she was a teen. After reading every Victorian Romance in her public library, she decided to start writing them herself —which she's been doing ever since. Faye lives with her husband and young son in England. She loves to travel throughout her country, dreaming up new plots for her romances. She's delighted to join the Tica House Publishing family and looks forward to getting to know her readers.

contact@ticahousepublishing.com